How I Came to Know Fish

Ota Pavel was born in Prague, Czechoslovakia in 1930, the son of a Jewish travelling salesman. Much of his family was arrested and imprisoned during the Second World War while he remained with his mother (who was not Jewish) in the Bohemian town of Buštěhrad. It is this terrible period in Central Europe's history that this is the focus of his most memorable work. Pavel worked as a sports journalist, both on radio and in newspapers and magazines and was himself an enthusiast for all kinds of sport, including ice hockey and fishing. While covering the Winter Olympics in Innsbruck in 1964 he became severely ill and spent much of the rest of his life in various mental hospitals, during which time he wrote the marvellous *How I Came to know Fish*. He died of a heart attack in Prague in 1973.

OTA PAVEL

How I Came to Know Fish

*Translated from the Czech by Jindriska Badal
and Robert McDowell*

PENGUIN BOOKS

PENGUIN CLASSICS

Published by the Penguin Group
Penguin Books Ltd, 80 Strand, London WC2R ORL, England
Penguin Group (USA) Inc., 375 Hudson Street, New York, New York 10014, USA
Penguin Group (Canada), 90 Eglinton Avenue East, Suite 700, Toronto, Ontario, Canada M4P 2Y3
(a division of Pearson Penguin Canada Inc.)
Penguin Ireland, 25 St Stephen's Green, Dublin 2, Ireland (a division of Penguin Books Ltd)
Penguin Group (Australia), 250 Camberwell Road, Camberwell, Victoria 3124, Australia
(a division of Pearson Australia Group Pty Ltd)
Penguin Books India Pvt Ltd, 11 Community Centre, Panchsheel Park, New Delhi – 110 017, India
Penguin Group (NZ), 67 Apollo Drive, Rosedale, North Shore 0632, New Zealand
(a division of Pearson New Zealand Ltd)
Penguin Books (South Africa) (Pty) Ltd, 24 Sturdee Avenue, Rosebank, Johannesburg 2196, South Africa

Penguin Books Ltd, Registered Offices: 80 Strand, London WC2R ORL, England

www.penguin.com

This translation first published in the United States of America by Story Line Press 1990
Published in Penguin Classics 2010

Set in 10.5/13 pt Dante MT
Typeset by Ellipsis Books Limited, Glasgow
Printed in England by Clays Ltd, St Ives plc

ISBN: 978-0-141-19283-3

www.greenpenguin.co.uk

Contents

Concert

For every fisherman, it is best to be initiated into the lore of fishing as a child by a father, an uncle, or a ferryman. In our case, it was the ferryman Karel Prosek from Luh-under-Branov, whom we grew to love as an uncle.

He not only taught me and my brothers Hugo and Jirka how to catch fish, but he taught my cunning Papa, too. Uncle Prosek knew so much about fish that he was probably born in the Berounka River like a water sprite and tumbled into Luh on the waters of a flood. He had a sonorous voice, a fine figure, and a beautiful moustache like a dragon. He could do anything in the world! He could plow and sow, milk cows, cook potato pancakes, find wild boletus mushrooms even out of season, ferry people in his boat during high waters, weave baskets, hunt deer, rescue travelers and half-frozen animals, silence the stupid, and he knew how to laugh. Many times, during high waters, he would ferry the mid-wife Flybertova and her indispensable suitcase. And he knew how to catch fish. Many ways! He'd impale them from his boat on moonlit nights with a fork called a 'grondle,' he would sink down weirs in their path, or he would cast out a line in broad daylight and catch them on a rod like a gentleman.

This was during the time of the old Austrian monarchy, when Count Max Egon Furstenberg lived in Krivoklat castle eating hot goulash and drinking Rakovnik beer. Because Prosek was the best fisherman in the region, the Count allowed him to fish in any manner he chose and in any part of the river. But if he caught eels, with their meat like lotus blossoms, he must bring them to the castle! He carried the eels in a sack, which his wife Karolina sewed from canvas. He carried them, still living, along the Berounka to the castle. The gates would swing open majestically, as if for a conquering knight. Inside, he poured them into a pitched cask filled with water, and sometimes received a gold coin. The coin had the emperor on it and resembled the sun.

But after the Count climbed into his carriage and disappeared behind four foreign rivers, Prosek was forbidden variety in his manner of fishing. The rod, he was told, would be sufficient for all.

Prosek had a long, yellow bamboo rod, a whip without a spool. He would walk against the rushing water so that the fish could not see him and crack the whip as he styled his dragoon's moustache. That is how his method got the name 'crack-casting.'

One day we drove up in our car, my Papa Leo, my Mama Herma, my brothers Hugo and Jirka, and myself, our whole family. From under the alder trees all of us were watching Prosek on the far side of the river. He moved across the slippery stones like an otter. His floater flew to the exact spot he aimed at. And the fish? They seemed to jump out of the water – silver chubs with red rudder fins, elegant whiskered barbels, big-bellied roaches from the tide pools, and daces from the swift currents. All of them slipped into his net, their freedom over, their master come, the King of Poachers.

My Papa, ever enthusiastic, cried out, 'Herma! What a concert! Just like Kubelik.'

Suddenly, I imagined rows of theatre seats along the shore in which gentlemen in English checked plus fours and ladies in pink crinolines sat sighing and applauding as each fish was caught.

Messieurs, mesdames, this is true art. In his over-flowing net Prosek caught up the last fish, then lit a cigarette and bowed.

The vision faded and Prosek was wading the shallow river towards us. Papa had immediately taken a liking to Prosek, because he too was a smart fellow. He could silence the stupid as well as Prosek could, and what he could not do Prosek would teach him. Ruffian Prosek suited my father well because his whole life he maintained that fine people are not worth shit. Papa and Prosek agreed that we would come to his ferry house for our summer vacations and his house alone.

My First Fish

Prosek returned from the Anamo pub in high spirits, singing old army songs. He knew a lot of them, having fought during the war in Serbia and carrying still a fragment of shrapnel in his hip. This souvenir often pained him, but he claimed that it stopped hurting once he had several hard shots inside him. In this condition he arrived at the boat, kissed the Alsatian, Holan, on the snout and sat down under the sweet-smelling acacia.

I was at the ferry at that time because my brothers did not take me with them again. They preferred the company of Dasa, the daughter of Beda Peroutka, who ignored me.

Prosek looked at me with his green eyes. 'Come here, Jackass!'

I dragged myself slowly toward him. He did not love me much. His favorite was Jirka, a scoundrel after his own heart. I was the youngest, only a pet. Prosek stared at me and pulled out a pickle from his dirty pocket.

'Here!'

I took my finger out of my mouth and put the pickle in. Prosek watched me. Then he pulled out his flask.

'Drink some!' he commanded.

The bottle was empty, but I made a blissful face. The non-existing alcohol brought us together. When he got up to go to the barn, he motioned for me to follow him. Inside, he drew out a long hazel twig.

'I'll make you a rod,' he said. 'I've been saving this twig for you for a long time.'

Unsheathing his sharp pocketknife, he cut here and cut there. Fascinated, I followed his calloused hands, noting the one finger he was missing, which he had cut off while slicing twigs for baskets. I looked up at his face, the contortion of pain on it, and realized that the shrapnel in his hip must be flaring up again without booze to keep it cool. Despite the pain, Prosek finished my rod. At that moment, I had no idea that it would be the most precious rod that I would ever own, but I know it now. It was my childhood rod, unparalleled even by the advanced American and Japanese models I would covet in later years. Prosek strung a line to it, then added a goose quill and a hook.

'Near the island,' he said, 'you'll find perch. Go, Jackass, and ruffle their feathers. I'll wait for you here.'

Before running out of the barn, I turned back to see Prosek curling up to sleep with Holan's head in his lap.

Following the path to the island, I reached my

destination before noon. The sun was already quite warm. I baited the hook with a plump earthworm and cast the line, but nothing happened. The fish would not bite. Only bluish dragonflies sat on marsh marigolds while somewhere in the backwater chubs were snacking contentedly. The white quill lay upon the water like a sailboat on a dead sea. In my mind, I hoisted the sails and ordered the captain to get under way, and we were pulled across the drowsy surface by a colored fish. But the quill, in fact, was still. My eyelids grew heavy, but I managed to blink from time to time with one eye to see if my white ship had set sail.

Suddenly, the quill shook and a circle appeared around it. And again and again, as if signaling or flirting with my ship, as if the engine crank were being turned. So it was not a sailboat, but a white motorboat. Then it hopped, stood on its head, and put up its feet like a half-submerged duck. By then I was wide awake and holding the rod firmly, expecting at any moment the sight of a wild-maned perch. But the quill made a JUMP! and disappeared. I could see it racing under the surface towards the marsh marigolds. The rod bent into an arch, and for the first time in my life I felt the delicious pull of a fish. After a tremendous battle, a bristled mouth appeared. It was a perch all right, as big as a checked red cap, but it was also olive-green with dark stripes across it. The fish carried its red fins like flags of war, and with its hump it resembled a bull. Instead of eyes, I gazed into live gold coins, and spears seemed to protrude from its back. This was no fish! This was a dragon, or an armored knight with a red plume jutting from his helmet.

I hauled the fish onto the grass and lay on it so that it could not escape. We fought like two boys, then I carried it ceremoniously to the ferry. I had pricked myself on its spears, and there was blood on my fingers. I thought that from this day forward Uncle Prosek would care for me as much as he cared for Jirka. He was sitting on a bench drinking milk – goat vermouth – to chase away the alcohol.

'You're a crackerjack!' he said.

Then he skinned the perch and nailed its head and skin to the barn door, announcing to everyone who could see that another fisherman had been born in Luh-under-Branov. I sat on a milking stool for days beneath my trophy. When somebody passed by on their way to the ferry, I would cough and blow my nose if they did not immediately notice the perch. I basked in the praise. Even Dasa, daughter of Beda Peroutka, kissed me on the cheek.

'You're the tops!' she said.

But one night my prize disappeared. Possibly the cat, Andelka, ate it. But it is more likely that my beloved Uncle Prosek removed it from the barn door. He had grown tired of my strutting about and was more than a little annoyed with me.

Battle for Pike

My brothers decided to accept me at last. We would catch small fish for bait, officially called gudgeons, but our name for them was chop, the same as a chop our mother would fry. The chop is a good-looking fish, almost marbled and with two blue fins. God must have had a good time making them, but the chop is a trusting and stupid fish.

To catch chops we would stir up sand and mud with our feet, which the chops explored for food. They found instead our lines and hooked earthworms. They pecked like hens, pulling the floats, then we would yank on the lines and the chops would come into the daylight. Now and then they swam between our feet and pecked at our toes. Peck. Peck. Peck. We splashed our feet in cool water and fished at the same time. We put them into cans and then Papa and Uncle Prosek would use them to catch pike and other water cannibals.

But then the chops became scarce in the river and Uncle Prosek discovered that pike also found the meat of the prickly perch delicious. Imagine! Perch on the pike's menu, and nobody had known about it before!

At that time Beda Peroutka, a typographer from Zizkov and a fan of *Victoria Zizkov*, visited the Krivoklat region in his old wreck of a car with his wife, Vlasta. My Papa quickly made friends with him, and each Christmas they'd exchange potato salad in painted chamber-pots. They were all so young. When we drove from Krivoklat back to Prague, pike hung outside open cabriolets; behind the cars trussed-up pots and buckets jiggled. Speed was not important. During the trip the crews shouted slogans and obscenities at each other, but the women did not blush anymore because they were used to it.

At Krivoklat, Papa was supposed to call, 'Here lives Holub the confectioner!'

Following in his car, Peroutka would happily respond, 'So bend and kiss the sweet spot, Bub!'

If my Papa forgot this ritual, Peroutka would sulk all that day and night.

Once in Luh, Beda decided to teach Prosek and Papa a thing or two about fishing and took off with Frantisek Pavlicek, the local champion, to catch pike at Devil's Rock. This fishing hole got its name, one story goes, because a gamekeeper once tripped over a rock and spilled his flask full of the Devil over it; another more sober version has the Devil building a bridge one night over the Berounka River, which would enable him to kidnap a daughter from the fishery. But as the rooster began to crow, the bridge was still not finished. The Devil was left empty-handed and had to stay on the rock. The pike, meanwhile, had always lived in the deep hole below the rock.

When Papa found out about them, he and Prosek armed themselves with beautiful perch for bait and steered their boat upstream beyond the island to the pike pools at Brtva. They caught enormous pike. One even had such an appetite that it jumped clear out of the water to get its perch.

They returned shortly before Beda, who when he arrived stood on the far bank chuckling and holding over his head a pike of at least two kilos!

'Beat this!' he bellowed.

'Come across, you fool!' Papa shouted.

Once Beda had crossed over, Papa took hold of his arm and led him to the creel. They peered into the box at the dark green silhouetted backs of three pike. Beda splashed himself with water so that he would not faint and tumble into the river.

'You bastards!' he gasped. 'You cheated!'

In the evening under the acacia tree, Papa confided the secret of the perch-as-bait and told him where to get pike the next morning. That acacia had such power that anyone sitting under it had to tell the truth. Even fishermen.

Under Sima's Rock

Time passed, and finally I received my first reel and wore my shirt tucked into my pants. Papa bought us a soccer ball like the one used by London Arsenal, that famous band of sharpshooters. At the playing field, we used it to fight many battles. In one of these wars, the boys dislocated my finger with a blow, and Uncle Prosek put it right again with one pull.

Meanwhile, the river was full of fish. We caught them, and Mama breaded and cooked them like steaks, or else she marinated them in vinegar with layers of onion slices. They were stored in a stone barrel down in our cold cellar. Delicious. When someone got sick in the village, the sufferer would come to our house for pickled fish. Those who were not sick came also. But those who most often came for pickled fish were pickled themselves – with hangovers! Ah, the fish were plentiful from spring until fall. They grew tender in the stone barrel and their bones got soft. They were cold in the summer and warm in the winter.

Life was a carnival. A red clay formation rose high

above the dam, and it was called Sima's Rock. Perhaps because a lot of Simas lived in the villages scattered around its base. Whenever we walked past the rock we sang:

> *At Sima's Rock*
> *two tramps sat back*
> *with no tough nuts to crack.*
> *So they played guitars –*
> *mcajcajcajcara,*
> *mcajcajcajcara,*
> *mcajcajcajcara,*
> *juchy, juchy, juch.*

Uncle Prosek in his straw hat would lead the way, then Papa with his fantastic mane of hair, Hugo, Jirka, and I would tag along. We carried long rods whose tips reached to the stars in the night sky. Our rods were so tall that I imagined us thrusting them skyward to light a star as one might light a gas lamp on the streets of Stare Mesto. As the sky darkened, the water below us tumbled down from the dam, which hummed as white whirlpools frothed and bubbled at its base. On the other side of the river, the mill at Nezabudice ended its daily rattle. From within the mill we saw one large white star, the window of the miller, Cech. And the sky and the vast universe spanned above it. Prosek turned to us.

'Let's stop here,' he said.

We had found the spot where the river was fast and

the barbel, that acrobatic strongman of fish, feasted. These belligerents live their lives fighting the current, disdaining the eddies and tide pools. They turn up stones with their snouts, hunting for small, delicious crabs and other tiny good things to eat. With their powerful fins and cylindrical bodies, they look like supersonic jets.

We stopped and unwrapped our tackle. Instead of lines, we tied long thin brass wires to our rods, which cut the fast water like razors. We put earthworms on our hooks. We settled into the soft grass, balancing our rods, and Uncle was the first to land a barbel. The fish bucked in the grass, cracking its four whiskers; it whistled and cried a little, perhaps was angry too.

Then a barbel snatched my hook and ran with it, the sound of its striking rising from the water like a cry heard from an enormous distance. I felt its weight and thought for a moment that I might have hooked some floating water grass. I yanked once on the line, and a barbel broke the surface of the moonlit water. It shone like melted silver, or like one of those pewter jugs used to pour wine from the royal vineyards. What a brave fish! It struggled against my maneuvers, fighting all the time to reach the safe currents downstream, fighting like a brave sailor who will not be denied the sea. Though we fought for every inch of progress, my line was like steel. And in the end, the barbel lay on the dewy grass, a victim of unequal forces. I patted his puffing sides as I might pet a dog or cat; I stroked his strange, cold, fishy body, then stabbed its head with my knife because even the brave must pay for their mistakes with their lives. I killed because I saw my Uncle Prosek and Papa do the same thing, just as they had learned by witnessing their ancestors work. The powerful fins of the barbel collapsed and what in life had resembled a beautiful airplane on a long-distance flight was extinct.

How Father and I Served Eel

My sly Papa had devised a daring new plan to capture eels. He decreed that we would lay down our line in the deeper currents under Palouk. We would stockpile our bait in spots where the eels were known to swim against the current. According to Papa, we'd serve them a feast they couldn't resist.

'We'll have so many eels we'll have to hire a butcher to smoke them,' Papa said. 'Smoked eels are best, for you can eat them all year.'

Papa also said that we must wait for the right time. Not until the moon disappears, the sky fills with clouds, and the stars sleep. Then, too, the river must rise a bit and turn murky.

While we waited, we made our frantic preparations. We cut up two new laundry lines; with a file we sharpened the tips of our hooks so that they would penetrate the eels' snouts. And we gathered bait. Down at the brook we netted lovely small minnows. The males puckered their bloody red lips, and their bodies were smeared with green, velvet, and black. These fish looked like they belonged in an aquarium.

We hoped to serve up something not easily found in the river, and Papa declared that the eels would shit with joy. Then in Luh we almost destroyed Uncle Prosek's garden, digging to find a few rain worms. We were well equipped and ready when it was time to go.

When it started to rain heavily, Papa rubbed his hands. The water turned the fields to mud and swept drowned worms, soaked grasshoppers, and swollen aphids down to the river. The fish were stuffing themselves. Then the first dark water appeared along the shore. Just then some visitors came to the ferryhouse. They were cheerful, drying themselves in front of the stove, but Papa didn't want to talk in front of them. From time to time, he winked at me as if to say that the right time was fast approaching.

Finally, we slipped away at twilight, snug in our rubber boots and coats, and with hope in our hearts. We walked against the current, many meters above the river on a path better suited to goats than to people. I don't know how long we walked, but it was horrible. We slipped on stones and skirted deep precipices. Branches whipped our faces, and the rain poured down. Eventually, I could feel myself getting angry with Papa, who would look over his shoulder every now and then and mutter something like, 'This is the right time!'

It is a long way to Palouk, even in daylight. Everybody from Luh would agree, even the Vlks and the Pavliceks. I couldn't understand why Papa hadn't simply dropped our lines at the ferry, since no one would go to the river in such bad weather. But that was how Papa operated. He wanted *deeper* and *stronger* currents. After what seemed like forever, we stopped at Palouk. Papa put down the box of minnows and pulled our lines out of the rucksack. He turned towards me.

'Beautiful night,' he said again. 'They'll go crazy over this.'

I could see that Papa was possessed by the true poacher's passion. He alternated the bait, impaling a worm, then a fish, then another worm. He seemed to lose sight of me as he worked, though I stood there shivering. I began to feel that I couldn't care less about the eels. Even smoked ones. Papa finished what he was doing.

'Undress!' he commanded.

As I stripped, I stared at the river. At its edge the moon's reflection showed me that the water was rising. I saw the blades of floating grass rise and fall, the stalks bending then moving down into the current.

'Papa, the river is rising,' I said quietly as I took off my pants. He didn't react at all to what I'd said. Stark naked, I stood on the shore. God knows why, but I was trying to cover up my privates.

'Take that line to the river,' Papa said. 'When it's tight, drop the stone.'

I just stood there. I heard the river roaring, and I was terrified. I stood like a mule that is forced to go where it doesn't want, but I didn't have the strength to refuse.

'Go,' Papa said. 'Don't be afraid. You are my son.'

I picked up the stone and stared at him. I think he was beginning to get scared, too, but he also didn't want to lose his investment. After all, it wasn't easy catching minnows for bait. We had almost destroyed a garden, and we'd cut up two laundry lines. Papa had talked so much about eels that he didn't want to give it all up now. He didn't want to admit that we had come too late, that the water had already risen.

I stepped into the river. The first sensation wasn't bad. The water tickled my calves, my knees. It flowed gently along the shore, then hurried off into stronger currents. When it reached my hips I could feel its tug and pull getting stronger. I had to duckwalk more and more among the stones in order to stand up against the current. At the same time, I was still holding onto this large stone with a limp line tied to it. I could still see Papa's silhouette on the shore, and I heard him calling to me with encouragement, shouting as he did when I played soccer and, later, hockey. Still, I felt deserted. The water was up to my belly button, then my chest, and it wanted to pull me under.

'Go farther!' Papa shouted. 'You'll be there soon!'

I looked but couldn't see him any longer. His shadow had blended in with those of the trees on the shore. What right did he have to make me do this? He couldn't even swim! Mama had told me that was why he would never bathe with us. Imagining those eels must have blinded him.

The river climbed up to my shoulders, then to my neck. I could feel its power now. It wasn't the same river that it had been the day before. Now it was a killer. It dragged me off in its waves and shouted *Impudent Boy! Why did you come?* I managed a single cry.

'Papa!' Water filled my mouth, and I was losing touch with any firm ground underfoot. Luckily, I remembered that I must not let go of the line. If I did, I'd be torn apart by the stones and current. I freed the stone from the line and dropped it to the river's bottom. Convulsively, I clung to the line, and I felt something pulling me toward shore. Papa's shape reappeared to me as he slowly reeled me in to the safety of shallow water, the biggest creature he had ever landed in his life.

Stumbling into the bushes, I relieved myself out of fear and the cold. I heard Papa packing the line, removing the bait and cleaning up.

'My dear fish,' he mumbled. 'It wasn't quite right tonight, but next time we'll serve them until they shit!'

Squatting in the cold, I thought of how we had been driven crazy. Maybe the eels had been protected by their mother – the river.

The Most Expensive Fish in
Central Europe

Before the war, my mother longed to visit Italy. It was
not for the sculptures of Michelangelo or the paintings
of Leonardo da Vinci that she wished so much to go
there; she yearned to bathe in the warm sea. Mother,
you see, came from Driny, near Kladno, which offered
only a poor duck pond that was coated with dense
green chickweed, so she never got to swim much in
her youth.

Every spring she would ask father, 'Leo, dear, shall
we go this year?'

Papa would fudge by suggesting that we might
not have enough money, that we could have more
fun for less on the Berounka at Krivoklat. He had
different concerns. Business and fishing were his two
great passions. He excelled unbelievably in both,
preferred fishing, and considered it a disaster if he
could not combine a sales trip for the Swedish firm
Elektrolux – for which he sold refrigerators and
vacuum cleaners – with a fishing adventure. Very
often he would disappear from a business trip to go

fishing on the Berounka with his best friend, the ferryman Karel Prosek.

Papa's love of fishing reached its height when he decided to buy us a pond stocked with carp. We would not only enjoy the carp ourselves, but we would make a lot of money when we sold off the surplus catch. Mama looked at this whole business skeptically and warned him not to do it, but Papa shouted at her and she gave up. After several moments of silence, she muttered that the money for the carp pond might be better spent on a trip to Italy. Father did not say a word, but gave her a look of dejection. After all, he was sure that he understood business better than Mama did, better than all of her Christian relatives together! Later, Papa gave her a look that he assumed held a thousand years of ancestral wisdom in it, and explained that with the money they would make on the carp, they could all go to Italy. Even Mama's relatives. I must point out that this was what Mama feared the most!

Nevertheless, Papa was in the market for a pond, a very particular pond. This pond of his soul would be surrounded by leaning willows and marsh marigolds with yellow blossoms, and basking in its waters would be carp the size of calves. Drawn to this vision like a bee to pollen, Papa made many excursions into the Czech countryside in search of a pond, but he found none for sale. But one day in Krocehlavy Papa saw his old acquaintance, Dr Vaclavik, a big, strong fellow with a moustache.

He said to Papa (who at that time had the title of

Inspector for God knows what reason), 'Inspector, would you like to buy my fish?' Papa was clearly startled. 'How much would it cost, Doctor?'

'Ten thousand. I'll show you the bill so you can see how much I paid for the little carp years ago. Naturally, they've grown considerably since then. You'll see!'

'I believe you, Doctor,' Papa said.

'Come, at least let me show you how big they are.'

As they walked to the pond, Papa had a gut feeling that *this* was *it*. It was the same unfailing intuition that told him where he would sell a refrigerator or vacuum cleaner, or tell him when ringing a doorbell or knocking on a door would be in vain. And as he'd learned to follow his nose in business, so he knew he was following his nose to his chosen pond of big-bellied carp.

Just as the dam came into view they stopped. The two men delighted in the scenery. The pond, rectangular in shape, was not too large. Lovely light green willows lazed along its banks, soaking their branches in calm water. Yellow blossoms of marsh marigolds floated on the pond's surface. Papa sighed.

'And now the carp,' Dr Vaclavik said emphatically.

Removing a bun from his pocket, he broke it in two and threw half of it toward the dam. He turned with a confident smile toward Papa, who intently followed the floating bread. Suddenly the water's surface parted, a large yellow body appeared, and a gigantic jaw clamped shut on the morsel.

'Jesus Christ!' Papa groaned. 'That one's five kilos at least!'

'Six,' doctor said meaningfully.

That did it. Papa rushed home to collect our savings. Mama consoled herself thinking that at least we would have our own pond with carp in it. Indeed, the pond's only disadvantage was that it was far away from Prague.

From that day on, Papa experienced a long period of extraordinary happiness. Sometimes he smiled absentmindedly, and Mama said that he was daydreaming about his carp in Krocehlavy. She understood papa's weaknesses, and so she resigned herself to endless discussions about the growth of carp.

Papa rubbed his hands and said to her, 'Herma, darling, we'll make a mint!'

At that time I had no idea what 'making a mint' meant, but I knew that it had to be something beautiful and big because Papa smiled and caressed Mama's hands. As fall bore down on us, we anxiously anticipated fishing out our first pond. We looked forward to it as a great holiday, especially Papa. He asked the Director at Elektrolux for some time off.

'Fishing again?' the Director said. 'Fishing will be the death of you, Inspector.'

Meanwhile, Mama bought an elegant worsted coat to commemorate the occasion. She also invited her brothers-in-law, Karel Kopriva and Karel Hruza, two strong buckos whose precise task was to guard the dam so that none of the fished-out carp would be stolen. They arrived at the pond with their families.

To spearhead our assault on the carp, Papa hired a

Mr Stehlik from Smichov, a professional fisherman. He showed up with a crew of eight. All of them were outfitted head-to-toe in rubber suits. Mr Stehlik, strong, old, and experienced, desired order, and what transpired along the shores of that idyllic pond resembled a military campaign against an unknown enemy. Two five-ton Praga trucks with oxygen tanks and barrels for the transportation of the carp were parked atop the dam, while below them the rubbermen quietly spread their nets.

As the water was draining from the pond, Papa entertained visions of the wealth resulting from the sale to the Vanha company of the captured carp, and he treated us to two cases of beer and sausages and buns. For lunch Papa then took us to the restaurant at Nejedly's. After more beer the mood brightened considerably. Only Papa didn't drink at all, because he had never been much for drinking.

Back at the dam by three o'clock, we found that hundreds of spectators had gathered as the water drained steadily. At last, with very little water remaining, Mr Stehlik ordered the grand attack. One fisherman blew on a golden trumpet and all of them started to pull. The huge net bent into an arch, its cork floats bobbing on the surface like little ducks. Mr Stehlik shouted commands and his rubbermen, like puppets on strings, moved their arms back and forth. The tension in the audience rose as the grand finale approached. The carps' area narrowed to a small circle. At any moment the waving and thrashing of fish should appear, but nothing happened. Papa, who knew this fishing phenomenon, grew pale as beads of sweat popped out on his forehead. The fishermen pulled the circle of the net ever tighter until the corks bumped into one another. Obviously, the net was empty. But wait! At the muddy edge of the pond, in a shallow puddle, something was splashing. Mr Stehlik scooped it skillfully into a small handnet and held it up. Carp! And what a carp! Papa recognized it, groaned, and then everybody roared with laughter. Everbody, that is, except Mama and Papa. For Mama it must have been especially difficult. She had lived long in Drine, but Krocehlavy was her birthplace.

She hugged us close to her and whispered, 'My poor children. If only you knew what kind of a father you have!'

Papa, meanwhile, ran down to the pond. He studied the gasping carp as if he had never seen one before. Dr Vaclavik had not lied! The carp weighed even more than six kilos, having gained considerable weight since Papa had purchased the pond.

Papa turned suddenly and set out at a full gallop for the doctor's villa, intending to end this business with a thrashing, just as he had once seen the boxer, Frantisek Nekolny, do. But when he reached the villa, the maid answered.

'Doctor and Madam are vacationing in Italy.'

'Vacationing in Italy? And on my money!'

That night we had carp for dinner. Naturally, Mama would not speak to Papa, but when he boldly announced 'since we paid for it, we shall also eat it, children,' Mama could not resist the snide addition that even Papa's kinsman, Mr Rothschild, would find it an expensive dinner. And she was right. On that night we probably ate the most expensive carp in Czechoslovakia, even in the whole of central Europe! In all, it cost Papa eleven-and-a-half thousand for the pond and its fishing out. As Mama said, we could have eaten live salmon imported from Canada for that.

Papa calmed down. He even gave up on the idea of flattening Dr Vaclavik in a boxing match.

Many years passed. Papa continued to sell vacuum cleaners and refrigerators and do his fishing on the Berounka. One day, while sitting in his office on Konviktska Street, who should knock and walk in but Dr Vaclavik himself! Papa went beet-red in the face, but resisted the impulse to beat the good doctor to a pulp. Getting control of himself, he noticed that his visitor had lost his moustache. Dr Vaclavik was effusive.

'Inspector, Inspector,' he bubbled, 'how are you? It has been too long!'

Papa thought of saying that he was fine, that he was still eating the carp that the doctor had sold him, but he resisted. Now that the man stood before him, he knew intuitively that a better opportunity for vengeance would present itself. His visitor explained that his wife was demanding a new refrigerator.

'I came to you, Inspector,' Dr Vaclavik said, 'because

I know you'll give me the best advice. After all, we're from the same region!' He smiled broadly.

'Of course, Doctor,' Papa said with enthusiasm. 'That's my business!' Then he launched into a rapid fire sales pitch. 'I recommend the GV model with the Platr-Munters system and the marble countertop, and it's yours for ten thousand three hundred and fifty crowns!'

Though Dr Vaclavik knew absolutely nothing about the miraculous Platr-Munters system, he nodded eagerly. Papa displayed the refrigerator professionally, and Dr Vaclavik was every bit the satisfied (and sold) customer. Best of all he liked the marble on the top. Then Papa took him back to his office for cognac, and they chatted like old friends.

Dr Vaclavik brought Papa up to date on who had gotten divorced, who had married whom, and who had been born and who had died in Krocehlavy. Papa told a few jokes about Mr Kohn and Mr Abeles. By the time the good doctor had sipped the cognac once too often, Papa promised him that the refrigerator would be delivered in three days, but he would have to pay immediately. Dr Vaclavik did not have that much money on him, but said he would drive to the bank. An hour later, he handed the money over to Papa, who gave him a receipt.

After the doctor finally left, Papa called Skvor, a warehouseman.

'Do we have a junked refrigerator down there?' Papa asked.

'Sure, we can find one.'

Then Papa asked Kucera to paint it after the insides had been removed. To this lovely empty box they attached the MADE IN SWEDEN emblem, with Papa recalling the pond in Krocehlavy and how it, too, had been so beautiful at first glance with the willows surrounding it and the yellow marsh marigolds floating on its surface. So that Dr Vaclavik's pain would not be too great, Papa asked that the marble top be included. The refrigerator was shipped to Krocehlavy.

Dr Vaclavik called in a mechanic from Libusin to connect the machine, but the mechanic walked out horrified, crying that he wanted nothing to do with it. The doctor immediately got on the phone to Papa.

'Inspector!' he shouted. 'This refrigerator has no guts! You sent me a box. Listen, I have a rabbit hutch already. I don't need another one!'

'Well, Doctor,' Papa said, 'nothing can be done. Think of your new refrigerator as I thought of my new pond. Both of them looked great on the outside but had nothing on the inside!' And Papa hung up.

Dr Vaclavik did not appear in Prague to settle the score with his fists. He did not sue Papa. But there must have been at least one sad night at the Vaclaviks, a night not unlike the one we'd had after fishing out the pond. Dr Vaclavik bought the most expensive rabbit hutch, not only in Bohemia, but in all of central Europe.

In the Service of Sweden

Frantisek Koralek, general manager of Elektrolux where Papa worked, was a wealthy man. His monthly salary was 30,000 crowns, he owned a villa at Ore-chovka, and bought a new American car every year; he had no children but he owned the Frako stable in Chuchle, complete with magnificent horses and English jockeys to ride them.

According to Papa, Koralek was a bigtime gangster. Papa believed this because he was convinced that his boss did not deserve his wife, Mrs Irma. Papa was very fond of Mrs Irma. She was Jewish and had striking blonde hair, blue eyes, breasts that stood out under suggestive fabrics like satin or shantung and would make a sculptor weep, and a firm, rounded ass. She moved as gracefully as the mares in her husband's stable, and her expression was intelligent and cultured. Her style impressed Papa, who never knew when to write 'i' or 'y' in even the simplest words. This problem of his started at an early age when he was expelled from school for a number of activities, his last rebellious act consisting of throwing an inkwell at his teacher, Lukes.

Mama knew about Papa's 'secret' torch for Mrs Irma, but it never bothered her much. She always thought that Papa's chances were as good as his climbing Mount Everest. After all, he had three sons on his back, owned neither horses nor a big American car, and knew only soccer, boxing, and fishing. None of these would dazzle Mrs Irma.

Papa's past was well known, too. Before he joined the famous Swedish company of Elektrolux, he had been selling Tutankhamen fire extinguishers for a local manufacturer. It was common knowledge that several factories burned to the ground while experiencing their prowess. Papa also let it slip out how we had lived at that time, and the news traveled fast through Prague. We had lived in a village in the woods near Marienbad and had eaten salted mushrooms and healthy onions without eggs and bread. But then a miracle occurred. From the moment that Mr Frantisek Koralek spoke – 'So! We accept you as a sales representative!' – Papa's lucky star was in its ascent.

His course was launched shortly after his acceptance on a trial basis at the Elektrolux branch office in Pilsen. His superiors entrusted him, with some hesitation, with one sample vacuum cleaner in a wooden suitcase, but they did not give him any spending money. So he had to walk with that suitcase all the way to Rokycany because he had no money for a train ticket. In Rokycany he loitered for two hours in the town square before he worked up the courage to visit his first client and utter the memorized formula he'd repeated all the way from Pilsen: 'I am a representative of Elektrolux, and I sell vacuum cleaners made in Sweden!' The man did not throw Papa out. He even bought a vacuum cleaner. And before the day was done, Papa sold four more! Not bad for a novice working a town where people stubbornly clung to brooms and brushes, which they'd used for hundreds of years, and in which a vacuum cleaner for two thousand crowns was considered a devil's invention and wildly extravagant.

From Rokycany Papa traveled on borrowed money to Radnice, where our uncle the doctor recommended him to his clients, and then on to Pribram. Everywhere he went he recited his sentence, then followed the demonstration of the instrument with smiles, flattery, and compliments. In ten days he had sold thirty-one vacuum cleaners!

In Pilsen nobody could believe it. They checked the facts and reeled him in to show him off in Prague as a sacred cow. As he walked the corridors at company headquarters, doors opened and employees pointed and whispered about him. He was escorted to the general manager, Koralek, whose light-haired, blue-eyed Irma looked dreamily at him and offered her hand.

'Congratulations, sir' she said.

Papa was transfixed. He knew that he had never seen such a beauty, and as he kissed her hand in parting, he stuttered from happiness. As he left the building, he promised himself that for this company, and this woman, he would summon forth all his powers in the execution of his job. And so he did.

Elektrolux was very lucky in hiring Papa. It didn't take long for them to realize that he was phenomenal at selling vacuum cleaners and refrigerators. Who can say why, but he was a genius in his field. It is hard to predict a genius in art, to say nothing of a genius in the sales of cleaners of dust.

Papa's eyes contained a mixture of gaiety, sorrow, and humility, but all of these were dominated by the charm of an elegant and attractive man. He was bold and persistent, but he never crossed the boundary into impudence and rudeness. Only a few wicked competitors employed the time-honored cliché – that if one threw him out the door, he would climb back in through the window. He soon became the national sales champion for Elektrolux. This was no small honor. Elektrolux had its sales champions all over the world, and they were just as esteemed by the company as soccer champions were by their fans. At an awards ceremony, general manager Frantisek Koralek presented him the first prize, a gold Movado watch with double casing and a memorable engraving. Mrs Irma took his hand again and said 'Congratulations, sir,' and smiled at Papa.

Somehow, Papa did did not catch on that there were limits to Irma's social smile. Encouraged by it, he proceeded to win yet another gold Movado watch with double casing, and it began to look as if he might become the undefeated world champion of Elektrolux.

And as he climbed ever upward, the vision of the beautiful Mrs Irma goaded him on.

Mama was also immensely satisfied that we were doing so well. Our apartment was furnished, we were able to dress up, we had a full pantry and could afford to buy at Lippert's delicatessen. And once we had everything we needed Mama told us, 'Boys, Papa will really start carousing now!'

And he did. He dressed like a dandy. He purchased an English suit from Meindl-Meceles, shoes from Popper-Krasa in Vodickova Street, and a homespun coat from Knize. Homespun was a very expensive fabric then, in part because it allowed for the following performance, which Papa carried out inconspicuously for customers and once for Mrs Irma herself. He would push a pencil into the fabric so that only half of it was showing, then pull the pencil out and note the looks of astonishment as the fabric shrunk back.

In addition to his fancy clothes, Papa had his hair cut and his face shaved by one of the best barbers in Prague, Mr Weber in the Alfa Arcade. Topping it all off was his purchase of an American car. True, it was not the latest model, but it was still an *American* car – a Buick with two sets of headlights and a canvas roof, six cylinders, twenty-six liters per one hundred kilometers. Mama nervously wrung her hands when she first saw it.

'Leo, dear,' she said, 'what shall we do with such a big car? Who will drive it?'

'I will,' Papa boasted, though he knew that when

he drove anything, it always ended in catastrophe. He well knew that the car was huge, because even Director Koralek did not have such a big car. But that was the point. Such a big car was difficult to drive, and so we hired Tonda Valenta as our Sunday chauffeur. Tonda was a tall, blond, sympathetic man, and he had the patience of a saint with Papa as he drove us through Lany and on to Krivoklat on our fishing trips. Papa would sit next to him, constantly coaching his driving techniques. Anyone else would have killed him, but Tonda Valenta merely chuckled. Once, Papa insisted that he drive through Lany.

'Tony,' he said, 'I'll take over here. I'd like to drive once around the president's residence.'

Mama protested from the back seat, but too late. Behind the wheel, Papa jumped the curb in front of the house and ground to a halt entangled in the president's green gate. We were towed out by oxen, and our American car said goodbye to Czech roads for some time.

When General Director Koralek found out about our Sunday call on the president, he smiled wickedly and asked my father, 'How is your Buick?'

'Wonderful,' snapped Papa, and for the first time he was really angry at his boss. Papa stared at the clean-shaven round face behind the desk, saw the face multiplied in framed photographs, and then saw more photos like them in every office shouting KORALEK KORALEK KORALEK! Papa simmered, beginning to hate the man he worked for. And the more his hatred festered, the more his sympathy for the suffering Mrs Irma grew. He worshipped her. But even though he owned a homespun coat and an American Buick, he was still only a traveling salesman. It's sad that Papa did not realize this.

Mrs Irma remained ever steady, buying things for her villa in Orechovka – little dogs, the most expensive Rosenthal and Meissen china, original Philips radios from Holland. She gazed down from her luxurious tower on the career of my wretched father knowing that he had a crush on her. Meanwhile, Papa had made up his mind. He would succeed as no one had before. He would go *higher, farther*; he would be the undefeated champion of the world! And he achieved just that. In the sales of vacuum cleaners and refrigerators, Papa surpassed his peers from fifty-five countries! For example, Elektrolux employed two thousand representatives in Japan alone, and all of them vied for the title of leading salesman. But Papa won it, beating out his competition, a man from Buenos Aires. Papa sold more vacuum cleaners than anyone in the world, managing unbelievable stunts in the process. He even sold them to farmers in Nesuchyne, which did not yet have electricity! Of course, he assured them that he would see to it, though he never did. Papa also sold a vacuum cleaner to his old class teacher, Lukes, who had been the target of his inkwell long ago; he sold a vacuum cleaner to Kralicek, the constable who once confiscated Papa's gun when he caught him poaching; he convinced Prime Minister Malypetr that he must buy a refrigerator, and he sold two of them to Dr Edvard Benes!

Papa was crowned world champion in the Alcron Hotel. Company President Venegreen, who flew in from London especially for the occasion, pinned a gold medal on Papa's lapel himself. The ceremony was filmed by the famous American Fox newsreel company, whose cameraman flew in from the United States. Papa flew in from nowhere, though he did take a tram with Mama. Our Buick was still in the shop.

The first course at the banquet was roast chicken, and it presented some problems. Everyone struggled initially until Papa picked up a fork – Mama could not stop him – and tapped on his glass with it. Silence fell on the assembly. Papa spoke.

'And now I'll show you how one eats in Bustehrad!' He scooped up the chicken in his hands, bit into it, and three hundred traveling salesmen followed Papa's example. Some of them even whispered words of appreciation.

'What a nice chap, that Popper.'

But at the head table a freezing silence fell. President Venegreen and the general managers poked at their chickens with forks and knives, and the Koraleks exchanged significant glances, which told Papa what they thought of him. His greatest fears were confirmed, when he stared hard at Mrs Irma. As a world champion, he might expect some special glance from her. She smiled, but her look was the same that it had always been, and her pupils reflected the roast chicken he clutched in his right hand. At that moment, Papa perceived the barrier between himself and Irma Koralek. It was a barrier that he, a traveling salesman, could never cross, not even if he sold a vacuum cleaner to God himself. Saddened by this discovery, Papa was not even cheered much by the ice cream elephants – which he loved more than anything – at the banquet's conclusion. But something unusual would occur later, which would give Papa a sporting chance.

The painter Vratislav Nechleba lived in Prague. He was our most famous living artist. To know him elevated one's social status, and to befriend him – but no mortal could hope for that! After all, Mr Nechleba was eccentric and did not make friends easily. It was this same short man with the long hair who approached Papa's booth of refrigerators at the Prague trade show and introduced himself.

'I am Nechleba.'

Naturally, Papa had no idea who he was. He only recognized boxing masters such as Hermanek and Nekolny, but he nodded anyway. He noted Mr Nechleba's half-shut eyes beneath thick eyebrows.

'I'd be interested in these monsters,' the painter said, smiling and pointing at the refrigerators. 'Come and see me at the Academy.'

So Papa took off for the Academy, where he spoke to the doorkeeper. 'You have a certain Nechleba here?'

'Yes, that's our professor. His studio is on the second floor.'

Papa climbed the stairs and rang the bell, and in a

moment the door was opened by the same short man with the long hair.

'Oh, it's you. You must wait a while for me to finish something.'

Papa sat down in a leather armchair, watching as the professor took up a brush and daubed at the face of a man who looked like a lunatic with inspired hair. Papa did not like the man in the painting because an inner restlessness radiated from him. Finally, Papa was sufficiently disturbed to turn from the face and look around the studio. He noted dozens of paintings on easels, on walls, and stacked on the floors leaning against walls; presidents, artists, financiers, biblical figures stared back at him. Their faces appealed to Papa with such force, as if they were with him and wanted to chat, that he felt he was entering a new world. He walked around the studio, recognizing his own world in theirs: he understood people. Every painted figure seemed real, as if they were about to step out of their frames, shake his hand and offer introductions. Papa even caught himself wondering to whom he would sell a refrigerator or vacuum cleaner and how he would go about it. He knew people, and he read in those faces their happiness and sorrow. A voice interrupted him.

'Do you like them?'

'Very much, Professor. I never would have believed that one could paint people so realistically.'

Papa, who had never heard of Leonardo da Vinci, Rubens, or Rembrandt, said this with sincerity. Then he began to talk about people as he knew them, and about their eyes when they were dying or killing someone. He talked about the small lame man in a Hamburg nightclub who threw a stool at a pimp. The stool knocked off half of the victim's head, and the brain splattered Papa. He talked about the eyes of his friend, Zuban, who drank his own urine as he fled through the African desert. Papa talked and talked, and the professor listened with the same interest with which Papa had inspected his paintings.

Then the professor led Papa into his apartment where he introduced him to his dogs, Helios the slim golden bulldog, and Sam the grumbling English mastiff. He showed off his parrots, who shouted at Papa, 'Give me a little ass?! Beast!' The professor opened the doors to his rooms, and he opened his heart, too, because Papa was a thief of hearts. It took him only an hour to possess the professor's heart with his sincerity and the ammunition he'd stored up as a traveling salesman.

At last the professor said, 'I'll take two refrigerators, one for here and one for the studio. And please come back to visit me.'

Papa would have forgotten the professor completely, but some time later Nechleba's name was mentioned over black coffee at company headquarters.

'He is my friend,' Papa remarked in a low voice full of significance.

It was as if a bomb had exploded. General Director Koralek gasped for air. But he had his doubts. After all, only a short time had passed since Papa had eaten chicken with his hands at that important banquet. Koralek had always had his own opinion about Papa's cultural status, and it lay behind his comment now.

'You must be mistaken. We refer to Mr Vratislav Nechleba, our greatest contemporary portrait painter. Painter, do you understand?'

'Of course, Director,' Papa replied. 'At his studio not long ago we discussed what human eyes can and cannot tell.'

'And what can human eyes say?' the procurator Gutova asked.

'Only artists can grasp that,' Papa answered gruffly. And with that he transcended them all. Nobody among them, not even the general director, could imagine what human eyes can tell. At the end of the session, General Director Koralek motioned for Papa to follow him into his office. He closed the door.

'Say,' he said, smiling affably, 'what if Nechleba painted my wife Irma?'

It struck like lightning. Jesus Christ! Why hadn't Papa thought of that himself? Why hadn't he ever thought to say, as he sat with the professor, that he knew the most charming woman in Prague? The professor would be stunned if he saw her. He would consider her the most beautiful model in the world. And Mrs Irma would be happy and grateful too. She would smile at Papa as she always had, but then she might go with him to a cafe, and somewhere else as well. Of course, Papa was too much the businessman to let the director see how much excitement his proposal had inspired. No, he would linger, sidestep, and stall to increase his worth. He knew he'd be better paid that way, so he sat and was silent.

'Did you hear what I said?' asked General Director Koralek urgently.

'I did, but it's not that simple.'

'I know that,' his boss replied. 'Nechleba sent a message to Bata that he does not paint cobblers, and he accepted three hundred thousand from President Masaryk for a painting. But understand me. I don't care about the money. If need be, I'll pay half a million.'

Papa's eyes popped out at this in spite of himself, for he knew well Koralek's stinginess. Papa studied his brown eyes and discovered in them the desire to own something that other rich people could not easily acquire. This man, who chattered constantly in front of his subordinates, didn't give a damn about art; he probably wouldn't even care about having a beautiful portrait of his wife, except that it would give him the opportunity to repeat one sentence again and again: 'Nechleba is painting my wife.' He could repeat that sentence at lunch, at dinner, and write it to his relatives in England and the United States. He could say it long after the painting was hung, and he could let it explode like a bomb at important gatherings. It was strange, but Papa got it into his head that the general director didn't really have a high opinion of his wife's beauty. Otherwise, he would not be willing to pay such an astronomical sum for the painting. This made Papa furious with Koralek all over again. Professor Nechleba will paint Mrs Irma, Papa thought, for other reasons, dear Mr Director. Her image must survive forever. It must portray her beauty as well as her suffering as a result of living with you. She should wear a bright blue dress to match her blue eyes, and the painting should rest in a heavy gold frame. Papa felt some relief thinking of this, and he spoke.

'I shall ask the professor.'

The next day Papa set out to see Nechleba. As he climbed the side stairs to the studio, he imagined how magnificent the world would be for him after Mrs Irma's portrait was done. The fact had not escaped him, however, that Koralek was still his boss. As he neared the professor's door, one thought began to bother him. What if Nechleba failed to capture Mrs Irma's beauty? Of course he had painted presidents and ministers, but to render the image of such a woman was something else again. Her soft hair and azure eyes, her full lips. But if Nechleba succeeded, what a portrait it would be! Papa could not waste another second. The door opened and Nechleba peered out.

'Ah, it's you, sonny. Why such a rush?'

Papa, elated by his vision of the professor's most beautiful portrait, knew that it would not be wise to exclaim, 'Paint Mrs Irma for me quickly!' Instead, he said, 'I just came to see you, Professor.'

'So come in and sit down,' the professor answered.

Papa sat down and looked around the room. The

professor was not alone, for a bearded model read a newspaper under the light of a kerosene lamp. The professor worked slowly, pausing to consider before each brush stroke. Papa watched him for a while, then looked around the studio again. As he had before, he felt attracted to the faces of men who looked as if they were marching around him like the apostles on the astronomical clock. One frowned, a second smiled, a third grinned. And each one he focused on looked him straight in the eye. He was playing a game, and he liked it. There was no end in sight. But suddenly Papa felt a chill. Christ! There was no portrait of a woman! He felt hot and cold all over. The professor did not paint women! Director Koralek knew it, and that was why he was willing to pay such a fee. From that moment, Papa sat in the armchair as if he were sitting on thorns. He no longer felt any joy gazing at the masculine faces around him. When the professor completed his day's work, Papa decided to ask him straight out.

'Do you paint women, Professor?'

'You know, old fellow, I don't care much for females! They get on my nerves. When they sit for me, they prattle on terribly, and when they are silent there is nothing to them.'

'But you don't paint them at all?'

'Well, yes, about once a year. And then only Lucretia, my favorite woman.'

Papa sighed with relief. There was still hope. One per year. His business sense told him to be subtle, as

43

patient as a gardener tending a flower bed. Selling the professor on doing Mrs Irma's portrait would be hard, harder than selling ten refrigerators. He thought that he should get a look at Lucretia in order to compare her to Mrs Irma. So far he knew nothing about Lucretia; he was too bashful to ask, so he decided to leave.

'Come again, Popper,' the professor said, for he liked Papa. Papa wanted neither pictures nor money for charity. The professor felt good spending time with him.

To Papa's great surprise and delight, the good lady Lucretia sped up her own demise by thrusting a dagger in her heart. When Papa heard the news and realized that she could no longer compete with Mrs Irma, he was so satisfied that he spoke to General Director Koralek.

'It will be possible,' he said, 'but it will take time.'

After this, Papa lived like a baron at Elektrolux. He was a steady guest for Brazilian coffee in the director's office. Mama and the rest of us were invited to various banquets. The incident with the chicken was quickly forgotten, and Mrs Irma smiled at Papa all the time. The Koraleks even invited Papa and Mama to their villa in Orechovka, and it was there that it happened. While Papa inspected striped scalares in the aquarium and Mr Koralek politely asked Mama about all of us, Mrs Irma quietly approached Papa.

'After Professor Nechleba paints me,' she said, 'we'll celebrate. Just the two of us.'

Papa was energetic beyond belief after that, and it nearly ruined us. Instead of selling vacuum cleaners and refrigerators to support Mama, three boys, and an American Buick (in the shop again), he visited the professor. He sat up with him for hours watching him work. Papa, who until recently had not known that oil paintings or live painters existed, now mastered theories of painting techniques! The professor acquainted him with a constellation of famous contemporaries. Papa memorized the professor's collection, remembered every person in every picture, remembered what they wore and what their expressions were. He learned that the professor had painted the editor, Boucek, in 1901, and the actor, Eduard Vojan, two years later. Papa also improved his knowledge of Persian rugs, and when the professor did not have time he fed the bulldog Helios, Sam the mastiff, and the parrots. Mama knew that all of this was happening because of Mrs Irma, and she grew ever more emphatic with Papa.

'Your newfound interest in the arts,' she said, 'has been going on for too long now. You're bound for trouble. I'm telling you! The children will have nothing to eat.'

But he couldn't stop. No way. He was getting close to realizing his goal, and he was very close to addressing the professor directly on the subject. On a wintry day when the sky above Prague was like cotton candy and the sun shone down on Hradcany, the professor was in a splendid mood. He sat sucking the tip of his little finger, which he liked to do, and Papa made up his mind.

'Professor, I have wanted to say this for a long time. I know about the most beautiful woman in Prague, and if you painted her it would make me very happy.'

The professor's look soured immediately. 'I am not in the mood,' he said. But when he saw how sad this made Papa he added, 'Perhaps later on.' And that was that.

At the time, the professor was still painting his Lucretia, a woman with black hair and a pale face, who could not talk or defend herself against the artist as he molded her to his ideal. She was beautiful, but it was an inhuman beauty, something which Papa never dared admit to the professor. It was quite possible that the professor loved Lucretia precisely because she was dead. Whatever the professor felt for her, it was definitely not the same love that Papa felt for Mama, or the idolatry he felt for Mrs Irma.

Winter passed, then spring, but Papa could get no further with the professor. Still, as a fisherman and businessman, he knew the virtue of patience.

Finally, as summer began the professor said, 'Popper, maybe I will look at this most beautiful woman of yours!'

Papa, who teetered on the brink of financial ruin and had exhausted his capacity for judging paintings, Persian rugs, parrots, and dogs, was mightily cheered by this. 'Soon?' he asked.

'In a short time,' the professor answered. 'When I finish . . .' and he pointed with devotion to yet the latest version of Lucretia, who for a change was thrusting an ornamental dagger into the right side of her chest. Papa had hated Lucretia during that year, but at that moment he forgave her everything. He knew that his victory was close at hand. He knew that the professor would look at Mrs Irma and Lucretia would be dead forever.

Papa victoriously announced to the impatient General Director Koralek, 'It will happen. Believe it, Director. He always inspects the subject before he paints her.' Koralek nodded enthusiastically and invited him to lunch at the Alcron.

Then Papa struck while the iron was hot. He involved our poor Mama in his plan, promising her that everything would soon be over. He suggested that we invite Professor Nechleba into the country with us. We would take him fishing at Rozvedcik. Mama would roast meats and bake the pastries and cakes. When invited, the professor eagerly agreed.

With Tonda Valenta we drove out in our Buick. While we stayed at the inn, Papa and the professor camped in a tent at the Berounka River, which was still clean and full of fish. It was June and the nearby meadow, the most beautiful meadow I had ever seen, was in blossom. The professor, though familiar with London, Paris, Amsterdam, and priceless collections throughout the world, had never spent much time in nature. He went into rapture over the Klabal's meadow.

He hopped around like a small child, observing the grasshoppers, beetles, and flowers.

'Oh, Popper,' he cried, 'it's a miracle! Nature is so beautiful! It looks like kitsch!'

Papa agreed. He prepared their rods and quietly prayed for an overcast sky with no moon and stars, and the fish biting like crazy. He imagined the professor's enthusiasm rising and climaxing tomorrow with the singular sentence, 'So bring that lady you mentioned.' Meanwhile, he carried out a plan he had never followed before, and which violated all fishing regulations. He had borrowed about twenty rods from his fisherman friends, and he stuck these into the ground all along the shore. He hung a bell on the tip of each one, as if he were decorating a Christmas tree. When the fish struck, these bells would ring. He positioned the professor on a decorative pillow in front of the tent, and Mama served tripe soup, a roast veal, ham, cakes, pastries, and beer. The professor kissed Mama's hand. Thirty years later he confessed to Papa that he'd liked Mama so much he'd thought of asking Papa's permission to paint her, but had been too shy to do so.

At last, the mild warm evening that fishermen love came. One could almost cut it and put it into a rucksack. God in his heaven looked down on Papa. The professor sat on a pillow in the darkness, sucking happily on his finger. But suddenly the heavenly silence was disturbed – *jingle jingle*.

'Popper,' the professor said, 'somebody is ringing bells!'

'I don't hear anything, Professor,' Papa said, who was fooling.

'What? You can't fool me. I have ears like an owl's!'

'You're right,' Papa said. 'Let's get out of here.' Papa led the professor down to a rod that was swaying and jangling above the water. The professor took it, gave it a mighty tug, and a fighting, floundering barbel as long as his forearm flew out of the river. It glistened like silver on the grass, as if the moon itself had fallen down. The professor, who had never subdued a living creature in his life, was hooked. He felt the thrill of the hunt, the ancient fire that had burned in his ancestors. That night, it may be that all of Papa's friends from the river – muscular barbels, slithering eels, smart chubs – came to assist him in the professor's initiation. They swam to Papa's borrowed rods, snapping up earthworms and fish bait, and the bells rang like they do on Corpus Christi Day. All through this concert the professor ran up and down the shore while Papa waited on him like an attendant at a shooting gallery, removing fish from hooks and baiting them again. Both men were happy. In the morning the professor smiled so sweetly at Mama that she brought out the tripe soup, the warmed over ham, cakes, pastries and black coffee. And, on Monday after the magical excursion, the professor granted Papa's fondest wish.

'So bring me the lady you wish me to see,' he said.

Papa behaved like one possessed. Calling a taxi, he rushed to the general director and insisted that Mrs Irma wear her blue dress. Papa's boss drove his American car to Orechovka to fetch Mrs Irma, who took an hour to dress, then had her hair done by Pohl, the national hairdressing champion. Meanwhile, Papa hurried home, put on his best English suit, and also visited Weber, his barber in the Alfa Arcade. His big day had arrived at last.

At two o'clock that afternoon outside the famed offices of Elektrolux, Papa stood beside the general director's American car with all the airs and appearance of an English diplomat. Mrs Irma wore her azure blue dress and snakeskin shoes. Papa could not take his eyes off her. The chauffeur opened the rear door, and General Director Koralek said goodbye as if he were sending them off on a honeymoon. On the drive, Papa made a move to hold Mrs Irma's hand, but she pulled away.

'After the visit, my dear,' she said.

They got out and climbed the stairs. Mrs Irma was pale and walked slowly, but Papa encouraged her with his smiles. Upon reaching the studio door he rang the bell, but nobody answered. He rang again, and this time the professor answered. When he saw who it was, he remembered that beautiful meadow and magical night.

'Oh, it's you, Popper?' he said cheerily. Then he saw Mrs Irma and remembered his promise. 'And you brought the lady.' Papa expected the professor to invite them in, but nothing like that happened. Instead, the artist stared and stared at Mrs Irma's face. He looked amazed and suddenly, almost in a whisper, said 'Turn around, Madam. I must see your other side.' Mrs Irma did as she was told. As she turned, you could see her gorgeous plump buttocks and slender legs which tapered down into high-heeled snakeskin shoes. The elaborate curls in her hair suggested a magnificent butterfly about to escape the musty stairway of the boring academy. Then the professor exploded with a cry that sounded like the wail of a pig-headed child.

'I won't paint this broad!' he howled. 'No! Not at any price! No, and no!'

Mrs Irma wept on Papa's shoulder all the way down to the waiting American Ford. As they drove off, Papa's greatest desire was satisfied – he held Mrs Irma in his arms. But the dream was turned inside out. She wept as if her heart were breaking, and he consoled her. He felt her breasts pressing on his chest; he stroked her hair, caressed her shoulders, her tears on his hands. But it was the first – and last – time that he would hold her that way. By the time she recovered, Mrs Irma never wanted to see my dear Papa again. She remembered how he had eaten chicken with his hands. She told everybody that she had always had a low opinion of Papa's intellect, that Professor Nechleba shared her view and couldn't stand Papa, and that was why he had rejected her.

I'd rather not talk about General Director Koralek's reactions. He wanted to shoot Papa because he had already informed his relatives and friends in Europe and the United States that Nechleba was painting his wife. A condition similar to a state of war broke out between our two families, and only Papa's status as the past year's world champion saved him from being canned. Papa grieved for a long time over his unhappy love for Mrs Irma, but he was consoled a little by the fact that, once in his life, he had held her in his arms.

The satisfied one in all of this was Mama. Her predictions that Papa could not conquer Mount Everest came true, our pantry started to fill up, and we prospered again. Papa gave up painting, Persian rugs, dogs and parrots, and devoted himself to his specialty, which he performed flawlessly – the sale of vacuum cleaners and refrigerators. Professor Nechleba was also satisfied, for he painted his Lucretia again. Many years after the artist had given Papa one of her portraits, Papa delighted him by giving it back. During the war a drunken SS officer with blue eyes and blond hair had torn her down and slashed her with a dagger, thus killing her a second time. Then Papa wept. He had forgotten Mrs Irma long ago and secretly loved Lucretia.

White Mushrooms

We went off to collect brushwood. Many walk in fear through the deep forest around Krivoklat. At any moment, a traveler might be confronted with mounted bandits from Tyrov, their crossbows ready. Here one might meet the brave Czech kings and their courts.

'Your Majesty, I come from Luh-under-Branov and they call me Jackass.'

In the forest one hears things – the crying of humans, the moaning of injured animals. One might see a herd of wild boar, or the legendary stag with the cross between its antlers. I myself quietly brought up the rear of the family procession so as not to miss anything. From her magnificent town, my fairy godmother held my hand. The leaves had turned yellow. Autumn descended, and in the tops of strong trees nesting birds squawked out their aggression. Somewhere among them the bird Noh resides. If I walked too slowly, he would swoop down and make off with me.

As we followed the valley trail, Jirka sang in his sonorous voice:

Gamekeepers met me,
and with them dogs, dogs, dogs,
and one was going woof, woof, woof,
and the other gruff, gruff, gruff.

During the woof, woof, woof, and especially during the gruff, gruff, gruff, Jirka trembled and panted. We joined in as we reached the forest's edge:

When I wander away from here,
I throw a rucksack over my shoulder
because, my loon,
you tired of me so soon.

'Stop!' Hugo shouted. Mama looked back from the head of our group.

'What is it?' she said.

'Look at the white hillside!'

'They're only stones,' Mama said, 'a hillside full of white stones.'

'No, they're not stones!' And Hugo ran up the hill. Half-way up he turned and shouted, 'These are mushrooms!'

We hurried up the oak-studded, rocky hill where hundreds of white mushrooms grew among the stones. Kneeling, we touched them; some were overgrown, some had brownish, cracked caps. These last looked as if they had grown there for more than a hundred years. Yet all of them were different, as if each had been created by a different painter. Some were thin, some chubby, and some resembled cute figurines, Mama's boys and handsome old men. Many got a kiss on their caps from us. We dumped the brushwood from our baskets, filled them with mushrooms, and still there were plenty on the hillside. My brothers ran off to Aunt Karolina's house to fetch more baskets, and we filled those up, too.

In Luh, we laid out the mushrooms on a sheet in the barn. We all left them there, but Mama stayed behind. No doubt she wanted to enjoy them. I thought she might be planning the mushroom feast of the Emperor Nero, who loved mushrooms no matter how they were prepared. But when I returned, I found her sitting there still. Her hands were buried in the pile of mushrooms, and she was weeping.

'Why are you crying, Mama?'

'When mushrooms are so plentiful,' she said, 'it means war.'

'That's a superstition, Mama. Aunt Karolina said that.' She had told us how thousands of white mushrooms had grown before the first world war, and that poverty and destitution followed.

The next year our homeland was annexed by the Germans. Sitting on a bench in Luh, we followed by radio the aerial bombardment of Warsaw. We heard the heavy German Junkers and Heinkels thundering over the city, and then the first explosions. I covered my ears and ran through the town, imagining that even here in Luh I could hear the bombs. Then I saw them falling. The first struck a cellar in which there was a barrel of pickled fish. The barrel cracked open and fish plopped in the mud. *Splash!* The second hit a ferryman's boat, sending its planks flying into the air like splinters. *Crack!* A house by the river burned and sank, while above a huge gray Heinkel flew by, a laughing pilot with a white skull and bared teeth at the controls. I saw the black crosses on the plane's wings, and its bombs fell among my fish in the river. In a moment their dead bodies surfaced, resembling the big white mushrooms with the cracked caps. They were the white of the white death notices hung in the shop windows. And on these notices it was written:

WE SHALL NEVER COME HERE AGAIN. THE
CHILDREN'S CARNIVAL IS ENDED.

Carp for the Wehrmacht

At the beginning of the occupation they confiscated Papa's pond in Bustehrad.

'How can a Jew breed carp?' the mayor asked.

Papa had loved the lower Bustehrad pond for a long time, as a man loves a young woman (now and then, he had loved young women, too!), even though it did not show itself off like so many ponds in southern Bohemia. No steam rose from it, no reeds flapped in the breeze and no gulls shrieked, but it was decent enough for a pond in the middle of town, with a brewery on one side, poplars on the other, and houses and cottages scattered here and there.

Papa had drifted on the pond in a washtub in his boyhood; his father had also manned a washtub on it, as had his grandfather and great-grandfather, too. It was a matter of blood, Papa's link to that pond. It helped, too, that the carp were delicious. They did not stink of mud, and Papa could sell them for extra money, which enhanced the salary he made from selling refrigerators and vacuums for that famous company, Elektrolux. Before the war, Papa would walk by the pond feeding his carp, like hens, with buns he carried in a paper bag.

'Here you are, boys. Here. Here.'

They would swim to him, their mouths gaping, gobble up the bread and *dash!* They'd execute elegant turnabouts under the water. Papa would also spice up their feed with spill-over from the brewery. They grew as big as plump cakes! There was no stopping them.

When the Germans came, they confiscated the carp like so many other things. But the carp were the only things that they could really take away from us. Papa had wisely said long before the war that all of the money in our family was spent on eating, drinking, and living it up. Mama reproached him on occasion, suggesting that *he* was the one who was living it up. But that wasn't exactly true. When he made good money, he gave us everything he could, like magnificent pheasants with beautiful long tails that would hang in the pantry beside hams we could slice as we pleased.

There were, however, also the days when the official thugs arrived to take away our furniture while we stood at attention. We three boys stood at attention on another occasion, too, when our national anthem, 'Where Is My Homeland,' poured out of the radio. One night, after we had gone to our rooms, the anthem sounded. Jumping up in our beds, we stood in our nightgowns and Papa proudly showed off his patriotic sons to our guests.

Papa loved his country, perhaps more than Mama who was a Christian. For her it was somehow natural that she had a homeland, while Papa and his ancestors had to search for hundreds of years before finding one. And so, instead of buying food and supplies with our last prewar money, Papa purchased a beautiful Czech bust. That was all we had when the Germans arrived. Wrapping up the bust and what was left of our furniture, we moved from Prague to Bustehrad to be near Papa's native soil and his only pond. When the mayor announced that they were taking that over, too, Papa's shoulders did not sag. He did not stoop.

'Do so,' he said, 'if you want to choke on the bones of my carp.'

The mayor's eyes got big, but he remained silent. He didn't want Papa on his conscience.

Not long after that, Papa and my brothers went to work in a Kladno mine. Papa rode a bicycle, and that squeaking machine seemed to sing such unusual songs along the way. One couldn't understand. They were truly very strange songs. Maybe there was in them the disgrace and revolt of one man. Maybe that bicycle sang what was happening in Papa's soul. One blow after another began to fall on him. We knew that he still visited his pond and his carp. Though we were short of bread, he fed some of our portion to his carp, perhaps hoping that no one would fish them out during the war and they'd live to see its happy end. Day and night, Papa walked to the pond. He was possessed by it.

Once, at the dam among the poplars, he was horrified to see four men in smart green uniforms standing along the muddy shore with rods in their hands. He walked toward them, fascinated, wanting to ask how dare they fish in his pond. The first slim soldier in riding boots turned toward him and Papa saw the Death's Head and laughing face of the SS.

'What do you want, Jew?' the officer said. 'Do you have an appetite for carp?'

Papa was silent.

'Come and get it!' the Death's Head ordered, and reaching into a bucket he tossed a carp in the mud between himself and Papa. The carp began to sink, dying, and all four Death's Heads were laughing. Then one of them suddenly stopped.

'Get lost, Jew!' he shouted.

Papa turned slowly, unafraid, and walked away erect as always. Even the Germans hadn't taught him how to crawl yet.

The occupation was bad everywhere, but in Bustehrad it seemed worse. The destruction of Lidice shocked the world. All of Bustehrad, along with my father, my mother, my brothers and me, saw Lidice burn. We heard Lidice shrieking from over the hill. I had always gone with Prihoda to school, and suddenly his place on the school bench was desperately empty. We used to play soccer in Lidice, Papa had buddies there, and small, light-haired Mama often returned weeping from her forced labor in the Lidice fields because over the graves the dense grass grew tall from the blood and bodies of the victims. We could never forget the destruction of Lidice. It remained in our hearts like a tick under skin, a tick with a black hooked swastika instead of fangs and legs. Papa was shaken after Lidice. His eyes were filled with that damned hundred years of sorrow, and he stopped going to the pond because he no longer believed that the carp would one day be his again.

Then another horrible blow struck. My brothers had to go to a concentration camp. That left just the three of us, and when we could we'd send them twenty-kilo parcels with special Terezin ration stamps. Papa would scrape up the money to pay for the parcels, and I would go to the farmers in Bustehrad and nearby villages to get food. I looked innocuous enough. I was weak and slim, only twelve years old. Nobody noticed me. There were wonderful people like the baker, Blaha, and the Burgrs, but there were others, too. In the winter I would walk from village to village, freezing with a small ruck-sack on my back, and knock at the large gates. At one farm, I waited in the yard for two hours before a woman brought me a very small bag of flour. I never brought home very much, but Mama would always praise me, stroking my hair and saying 'You are my little business-man.' And I was most ecstatic when I could beg a cigarette off someone. I would bring it home, then Papa would sit down opposite Mama and light up. Passing the cigarette back and forth, they talked about what life would be like when the war ended. Just before Christmas, Papa was called to the concentration camp.

We were badly off then, and Mama complained that she would not be able to give Papa anything to take with him. Two days before he was to report, he was shoveling snow in front of the house when a car pulled up and three civilians got out. This visit was not unexpected, for we owed some taxes to the Jewish district.

'Look, a miracle!' one man said. 'The Jew's doing some work!'

'While you're loafing about,' Papa said.

'Who do you think we are?' the man said.

Papa looked them over and noticed that one looked very Jewish. 'You look like the entire Jewish municipality,' Papa said.

One of the men concluded that this exchange had gone far enough. He pulled out a badge and showed it to Papa.

Geheime Staatspolizei. So it was the Gestapo, then, Papa thought, and he said 'Well, hello Kaiser.' Those Gestapo men somehow liked him, and the one with the mustache spoke up.

'Obviously, you are no shit-eater. So go inside and show us those hidden rifles and machine guns.'

They inspected the house and stopped, surprised, in the living room. Before them, in a Jewish household, stood a Christmas tree decorated with tinfoil. The man with the mustache even smiled a little at Mama. Then they climbed into the attic where they discovered, back in a corner, the wrapped Czech bust. The joking stopped, and the man with the mustache did not smile at Mama again. They made Papa carry the bust to a window and drop it to the concrete yard below. Then he was made to smash it to bits with an ax. When they left, Mama, who had experienced this before, said that one could still find decent Germans, but Papa only spat. The next day, we heard that those decent Germans had killed two neighboring Jewish families after they searched our house.

Because Papa had to leave in the morning, we celebrated Christmas Eve early. We lit the candles on the tree, the tinfoil shone like silver, and the room smelled like a forest. God knows where, but Papa had found me some old shoes with skates, keeping alive his dream that I would one day become a famous hockey player. From some boys at school, I had managed to get him two packs of cigarettes for his journey to the camp. Mama and Papa did their best to look gay. They hummed, hoping that I would have some fond memories of the evening. They must have felt horrible on what might have been their last evening together.

During the night, somebody shook me awake in the darkness.

'Get up, buddy, get up.' Papa was shaking me. I didn't want to get up because it was brutally cold in the room. My teeth chattered and I was shivering, but I managed to get dressed. In the next room, Mama helped me into a winter coat and hat. Something was up, and I had no idea what.

'Papa is waiting for you in the courtyard,' Mama said.

I walked down the stairs, and Papa stood there holding an ax and a bundle of sacks. I felt scared as he nodded at me. He started out and I followed, the hard snow crackling under our feet, *crack-crack*. Papa did not speak as he headed for the pond, which stood out behind the poplars, as if in a fairy tale, all frozen over and lit by the moon. There was silence, enormous silence everywhere. Near Hudecek's house Papa began to tap on the ice, walking far out onto the pond. The ice beneath his ax sounded like a church organ.

'The carp are suffocating,' he said, turning to me. 'Nobody cut holes for them.' Spreading his feet apart, he struck the ice. The sound rumbled through the night, and I shivered. 'We will do it here,' he said. He stood and hacked at the ice. Ice splinters showered his clothes and face as he cut out a square and pulled it out from the water. 'We'll have to wait, buddy,' he said. 'They'll swim here soon.'

I was mesmerized staring into the transparent water in which each crease and pebble on the bottom stood out. The water quivered with the life-giving bubbles from the air, and that square in the ice looked like a safe well for carp travelers. Papa understood it, and suddenly a dark, oval-shaped shadow swam under us. It returned. A carp. And what a carp! He stuck out his rounded snout and gasped for air as another arrived. They looked drugged, not minding at all that we were there and watching them. In seconds the carp filled the hole, and still more were coming. Then Papa was overcome by something deep and unknown. He knelt down on the ice and rolled up his sleeves. He stroked their heads and backs, mumbling 'My darling carp. Little carp.' He played with them, and they flocked around his hands like his children, gold and silver in the moonlight, shining like saints. I never saw such carp again. Papa rolled them over, lifted them, then let them go as he hummed something.

At last he got up, the moon shining in his face, with a look of complete contentment. He pulled a hand net from one of our sacks. Holding the sack open, he walked to the hole and scooped up the first carp. Only then did I realize what he was up to, and I was terrified.

'Papa, let's go!' I said, pulling on his sleeve. 'If they catch us, they'll kill us.'

His face was blank as he stared at me, and today I know that he didn't care if he were caught and beaten to death. He couldn't depart and leave his carp to the Germans. He didn't pet the carp anymore. We put them in sacks and carried them home where Mama separated them into containers. Our house was rapidly filling up with water. Carp swam in buckets, the bath tub, in barrels, and in old horse troughs in the stable. In the morning when the moon dropped low, it got even colder. We were frozen to the bone as we lugged the last wet sacks home. Mama scraped the ice from us, and we thought of the pond that was empty now. The carp had come home. Papa had stolen his own fish.

In the morning, we went to see Papa catch his bus to Prague. He carried a small suitcase, and for the first time his shoulders sagged. But to me he had grown enormously during that night.

Back home that day, Mama and I began to exchange the carp for food with the merchants and farmers. At Christmas the carp opened the doors of the most forbidding fortresses. The moment that I would show off a plump fatso in the sack, the housewives would rejoice. My cold room filled up with lard, smoked meat, flour, sugar, loaves of white bread, cartons of cigarettes. Several times I was invited inside to tables from which I could help myself to white coffee and Christmas braid. I did not have to wait long outside the gates anymore. I was as welcome as a good king for whom the carp had opened a road into the world. It was my most plentiful Christmas.

Well, the following year they arrived with nets to fish out the lower Bustehrad pond. Wehrmacht uniforms mingled with fishermen. The carp were to be confiscated by the German armed forces. I stood among the boys on the dam and waited to see how it would end. At the beginning there was a big celebration. A brass band played on the dam nearby, and all looked promising. But there was nothing in the pond, and nobody could explain it. Only I knew that the band was playing in honor of my father, who with David's star on his coat had stolen a march on the Germans.

The Death of Beautiful Deer

We three boys loved to go to the country around Krivoklat castle. Then I didn't know why, but today I do. Papa understood. Even then he knew that though one day I might see the boulevards of Paris and the skyscrapers of New York, I would never again spend weeks in a cottage where bread browns in the oven and someone churns the butter. He knew that one day cars would pull up at these cottages and TV sets would blink inside, and you'd be served bad black coffee and pale bread.

Long ago, Papa had discovered that region by following his nose. Back in the thirties, he drove by the castle with our chauffeur, Tonda Valenta, and followed the winding road west along the Berounka River. In those days pike the size of crocodiles swam there, and in the weeds of the shallows fat chubs and barbels as big as logs rolled about. Papa observed everything and pushed on to a roadside inn. It was there that we spent our first two vacation seasons. But it was not the place we wanted.

Though Mrs Frankova, a beautiful and pleasant

woman, cooked delicious goulash and tripe soup, the pub was far too rowdy on the weekends. Crowds of tramps, vagabonds, hobos, and cowboys raised so much hell in that pub that it was worthy of the Wild West. At first, Mama sent Papa to ask the tramps to hold the noise down, but she soon gave up. Not long after he'd go in to reprimand them as they sang songs telling how life was a dog, or how life in the Yukon without a woman was lovely, Papa's beautiful voice would join in. We poor children also heard the noise of the only instruments that Papa had ever mastered – a broom and pot lids borrowed from Mrs Frankova. In the morning Mama would find him, still drunk by the well, playing sentimental songs about his black Kladno on his comb.

Some lovely people, like Bambas the tramp, lived in that country. From spring to winter he never worked, but fished at Devil's Rock. To stave off hunger he'd slowly consume five lumps of sugar from a sack, which were left over from his last winter job. Bambas' life seemed charming to me. Even later on, when most kids wanted to become writers or pilots, I wished to be Bambas. He lived in a dilapidated hut and covered himself with a patchy deer skin. He could catch fish like crazy; he knew how in all the legal ways, but he mainly caught them in illegal ways. Mama didn't like it when I went off with Bambas. She was afraid he'd corrupt me. Unfortunately, he failed.

But I'm getting off the subject. About Papa and us.

After a wild night in the pub, Papa was forced to find us a farmhouse. Loading us into a boat, we sailed down to a small house under Branov. The ferryman, Karel Prosek, who wore a mustache like Hitler's, owned this cottage and we spent many happy holiday seasons there.

This magical cottage contained a real oven for baking bread, a cellar full of milk, butter, and buttermilk, a barn with a cow, a hillside of potatoes; it included woods full of mushrooms and clouds of fish in the clear water, which we could see from our window. It was paradise; the kind that Mr Werich and later Mr Matuska used to sing about. Papa could even wade into a sea of beer at the Anamo, the crossroad's pub.

Thanks to the industrious invention of Karel Prosek and my Papa's money, that cottage was soon transformed into the richest one in Luh. The cellar, for example, was packed with stone pots containing fish pickled in vinegar and onions; picking up one of these fish, the juices running down your fingers and small bits falling off, you would be delirious because it was so good. There were also pots of marinated venison. Long braids of Prague sausages from Maceska's hung from the ceiling, jugs of cream and cans of milk stood below. And there was always fresh bread and cake.

Papa also bought us an original yellow soccer ball. We played soccer in the open space, and from a wind-up record player which stood in the window of our room came:

Behind the wheel always going forward,
Somewhere in the distance is our goal.
Only strong nerves will overcome
dangers of thousands of miles.

Karel Prosek mysteriously stocked up on venison from Krivoklat's woods. I say *mysteriously* because for a long time nobody knew how he did it. Of course, the blood of poachers had pumped in Prosek's body since birth. His grandfather had been famous for poaching with great style. One day, he bet that he could sneak the strongest deer from Krivoklat past the police station at noon. He won, too, by placing the deer in a coffin and driving it by in a hearse! On another occasion, Prosek's mother had rocked a deer in a cradle while the police searched their house. The cops never forgot these escapades, for everybody heard about them, Karel was smart enough to know that he'd never get away with firing even a single shot again, so he threw his gun in the Berounka above the lock.

He had other plans. My step-uncle, Prosek, whom I'd rather follow into the woods than any of my real uncles, got hold of an Alsatian puppy from a farmer named Novak. He called the puppy Holan after a famous Prague moving company. The name suited him, for he could easily move furniture. Holan had a powerful chest; he had strong legs and an enormous muzzle. His nose protruded from his snout and his yellow eyes looked reflective. There was something hidden behind them. Indeed, they were the eyes of a wolf. Somewhere in his family relations something had happened, and Holan was basically a wolf. Even as a puppy, a furry ball and all eyes, he was killing hens. *Woof, woof! Growl, growl!* But mainly *jerk* and *pull* and *Death*. That came later. That is certainly why Mr Novak was happy to get rid of Holan. But Uncle Prosek needed exactly such a dog and was happy to get hold of him.

Holan would drive geese to the cottage, and one goose, which Prosek pointed at just before a feast day, succumbed to his jaws like a wild berry. He chased a cow and hens from the fields. Many mornings outside the cottage door, Prosek would discover a slain marten, skunk, and dead rat lying in a row like hens on a perch.

One day, we saw Holan attack a strong fox that was dragging a stolen duckling into the woods. Holan caught up with him on the hillside and lunged at his neck, but that fox was no amateur. For an hour or more fur flew and blood dripped as the tossing ball rolled toward the river. At last Holan, who knew how to catch trout, pinned the fox under water until it drowned.

Uncle Prosek and Holan developed a stronger bond, one for the other, than I have seen exist between most people. For love of Prosek, Holan would dive into water. Whenever Prosek refused to take him across the river in a boat, Holan would ignore high or muddy tides or floes of ice and swim out pursuing his master. Or when Prosek drank beer or rum in the Anamo, Holan would wait motionlessly for hours outside, his eyes never leaving the door.

Prosek always had a bad hangover. When he'd leave the pub he'd curse Holan and throw stones at him as the dog followed, just out of range. Prosek would curse the mortgage on his cottage; he'd even insult Papa. Then his delicate wife, Karolina, would ferry Prosek and the groaning dog over to Luh, and there Prosek would lie down in the grass under the huge, beautiful acacia, in whose blossoms bees buzzed in the spring, and sleep like one enchanted in a fairy tale. Holan, a nightstalker who never saw his master sleep in a bed, didn't understand this sleep and feared that his master was dying. He'd howl and whine, then snuggle up in Prosek's lap and put his snout to his master's nose. When he'd feel Prosek's breathing, he'd fall asleep, too. And when they'd wake up, Prosek would bellow 'Holan! You brute!' and stomp down to the cellar for cucumbers pickled in vinegar and dill. The next day Prosek would be hoeing his rocky fields while Karolina lugged her heavy baskets of grass and brushwood many kilometers from Brtva meadow. That was their life, but not quite *all* of it.

A strange slope rose above the river island. The stones, which usually pocked such projections, were not there. Instead, soft green patches of long grass grew among the big oaks. Game animals, trotting down to drink from the river, paused to graze there.

The slope looked like a beautiful garden or a castle park, but it was a garden of death. *The Death of Beautiful Deer*, one might call it. Some time back, Karel Prosek had taken Holan's head in his hands near here and pointed it at a brown dot on the slope.

'Run, Holan!' he commanded.

Holan, only a pup the day before, took off as if he had hunted all his life. Running against the wind so that the deer wouldn't detect him, Holan moved as nimbly as gossamer. At first he bounded along as if he possessed air cushions instead of paws, then he ran bent forward, and at last he crept low. He shot ahead, gaining a slight but important head start on the deer. The deer bleated, tried to recover, but was too late. Holan stayed at its side, then jumped for the neck. His heavier weight drove the deer to the ground and broke its neck. Then, with a fierce snap, Holan would sever the artery in the neck with his jaws. Before Prosek could catch up, it was usually over.

This happened quietly on the slope under the silent oaks, while the warden's marked trees and the game-keeper's house warmed in the sun on the plain above. Prosek would stuff the deer into an enormous rucksack, then skin him in the barn and burn everything else but the meat. In this way they had meat for a month, and they had small potatoes from a stony field, too, where they had to dig them up with a hoe. People did not think this a bad way to live, because they also longed for adventure (although they didn't call it that as city people would have).

This went on for some time, but finally the game-keeper began to count deer as well as trees. Somehow the figures never worked out! Then they remembered Prosek the poacher and decided to visit Luh. As Prosek ferried the gamekeeper, Novotny, and his assistant across the river, they saw Holan pursuing something on the slope. Novotny got right to the point.

'That dog is a poacher, Prosek,' he said.

'No!' Prosek insisted. 'He isn't! He just plays!'

'Don't give me that!' Novotny said. 'He chases game. He won't stay off their trails!'

'I'll tell you what,' Prosek said. 'I'll whistle, and before we reach shore he'll be waiting for us.' Prosek dropped the oar, put his fingers to his mouth, and whistled. Then he picked up the oar and casually steered along. Landing under the beautiful acacia, they were met by Holan, who stood on shore wagging his tail. 'Where is the cow?' Prosek said. 'Bring her home!' Holan shook his head, ran up the slope and on to the field as Novotny watched.

'No,' he said. 'He's no poacher, Prosek. He's a good dog.'

From that day on, life there was a carefree paradise. The song 'A Thousand Miles' played over and over on the Odeon record player. Deer meat in cream sauce with dumplings steamed on the table beside local Branov dishes such as potatoes and dumplings or buns greased with butter and mashed potatoes, called *bang*, baked in a pan. Jesus, those were delicacies! And then it was over because former lance-corporal Mr Hitler arrived, sporting under his nose a mustache like the one belonging to my beloved Uncle Karel Prosek.

Luh, in those days, did not have a public address system. Instead, our local cop, Karel Kovarik, banged on a red drum with blue drumsticks and bellowed the news. He was a sight in his Austrian cap and shabby clothes. Formerly a cobbler and now as deaf as two logs, he would carry out his mission and then beg us boys, 'Give me a crown!' Papa usually gave me a crown for Karel, who'd smile happily as he marched off into the woods toward Kourimec and Emilovna, banging his drum along the way. The deer got used to him and gathered along the roads to watch him pass. They seemed to know that out of such bedlam came only goodness. In the end, though, Karel must have gone mad, because he walked through the woods calling to the animals to give him a crown, too. And when that Hitler came, Mr Kovarik drummed the news: 'Hear ye, Hear ye! Notice is given that the Boehmen und Maehren Protectorate is established in this country!'

Papa took it hard that he could not go to Krivoklat anymore. If it hadn't been for Mama, who he feared only a little less than Hitler, he might have gone just the same. In the third year of the war my brothers, Hugo and Jirka, were summoned to a concentration camp.

'The boys need to eat before they go,' Papa said. 'Meat. I'll bring some fish.'

Papa wasn't allowed to bicycle anywhere except to

work, he wasn't allowed to leave his residence without a permit, and he wasn't allowed to fish at all. He couldn't fish because he didn't live on the Riviera, but in a protectorate watched carefully by ever-attentive policemen and the Gestapo.

So he went to see his good pal from Bustehrad, Dr Quido Jerabek, who certified that Papa was too ill to work in the mine for a few days. Quido, of course, had no idea that Papa was planning a weekend in the Krivoklat castle region. Though Mama cursed like a storm, Papa left our house #54 in Bustehrad without wearing a star, which he ripped off and stuffed in his pocket. On the rack of the bike he loaded his knapsack, burlap bags, and a creel for eels.

The first night Papa pedaled through Zehrovice and Lany by stars that gave off a different light than the one in his pocket, which said *JUDE*. As he pedaled on he thought of many things, of how the world was so mixed up and shitty, of how just a short time ago he had been driving around in his American Buick like a lord. Now he straggled along ditches on a squeaky bicycle like a poor Jew.

Papa turned down the winding road to Krivoklat and pushed the bike up the hill to Visnovka. Then he pedaled along the Berounka River, where the foam roiled in pike holes and roared as it had years ago, and snakes already crawled in the heat. The beautiful Cech's villa appeared, then the mill, then Prosek's white-washed cottage with its two windows and red roof. Papa felt the magnetic pull of the place, but he stopped under the blossoming acacia as the river rushed on between himself and the cottage. He had come to this cottage a hundred times before, but that time he thought its loveliness impossible to describe. He did not know why, but it was because he had not seen it for a long time. He'd earned this trip by pedaling his bicycle so far and overcoming the fear that had kept him away for years. He felt different, to be sure, much different than when he'd driven up in the Buick seated comfortably on his behind. Gazing at the cottage, he suddenly knew that it would probably still stand long after the Germans had vanished, that Karel Prosek would survive, and maybe Jews, half-Jews, and quarter-Jews would live on too.

'Ferry!' Papa cried, sitting on the ridge.

In the old days all of us would have rushed outside to celebrate Papa's arrival. Mama would jump, fully clothed, into the Berounka just for fun while Jirka the best kicker among us, would boot the yellow English soccer ball as Holan barked like mad and the notes of 'A Thousand Miles' drifted from the record player.

But on this visit the cottage was quiet, as if men nearby were already shooting. After a while, a man in a hat stepped out of the door and was followed by a large dog. Prosek got into his boat and rowed toward Papa's side. When Prosek recognized him, he warmed up like the sun. For the first time in their lives, they kissed each other.

Papa didn't sleep at Prosek's that night, but parked

his bicycle in the barn and carried rye straw in a basket to the island. There he lay down and covered himself with a raincoat. In the morning, Karel brought him a breakfast of milk, butter, bread, and fresh poppy seed buns from Mrs Karolina. Later, Papa dragged the water, catching small chops for eel bait, then he prepared lines and the creel. In Bustehrad some farmers had promised him pig meat and lard for eel. The nights were clear and lovely, but that was bad for fishing. Perhaps the poet's full moon frightened the eels, who would not bite. Papa, growing more depressed, couldn't sleep, so he busied himself with baiting hooks with small fish and earthworms. But each morning the slack lines taunted him. Papa beat his head and cursed the whole shitty world.

'Don't be sad,' Karel said, watching Papa cooking raspberry dumplings in the kettle. 'You'll bring home flour and butter instead.'

'Karel, my boys must eat meat again!'

'Mr Leo,' Karel said, 'I have none, but I'll kill the cow for you today if you want me to.'

At this moment, Papa's real motivation for risking all to come here struck him. 'Karel,' he said, pleading and commanding in the same breath, 'bring me a deer.'

'Ever since the Krauts came I haven't been in the woods with Holan. You may think me a coward, but I have six children, and there's a death sentence now for poaching.'

'Okay, Karel. Will you lend Holan to me?'

'I don't know if he would go with you,' Karel answered. 'He has never gone off with anybody else.'

'He'd go with me.'

'If that's true,' Karel said, 'you can take him.'

'I'll come for him, Karel, when the time is right.'

Prosek bowed his shoulders and walked off. Papa spread his raincoat over the reeds and lay down, peering at the hill through Grandma's opera glasses. One day passed, then two. No deer came. Papa drank milk, which Prosek brought up to him in a jug. Neither man spoke to the other, as if a barrier had arisen between them. No words passed but 'Has he come?' and 'No, he hasn't.' And that was all.

On Papa's last day he lay on the reeds, pressing the opera glasses into eyes red with tears of fatigue and anger. Nature, it seemed to him, had conspired against a Jew. He thought of the clear, moonlit nights, nocturnal water snakes, and now the oak forest so quiet not even a squirrel would show up. As the afternoon lengthened, his cap fell over his eyes and he drowsed. The opera glasses slipped down among the reeds. When he woke up, it was very late in the day, the time when insects fly away somewhere, and cows are chased home from the meadows. It was the hour, too, when fish started biting. Papa rubbed his eyes. On the slope across from him, a deer grazed near the water. Was this a gift from his Jewish God? Papa grabbed the glasses and studied the deer. It had magnificent antlers, more beautiful than all those mounted horns he'd seen before the war at Krivoklat castle. It was a divine deer. His huge head stood out from a strong neck, and his coat was all red and gold, as if he had strutted out of glowing hell and not from God himself.

After nearly drowning in the muddy backwater as he waded to the opposite shore, Papa appeared breathless and black at the ferry house. Prosek welcomed him.

'What are you up to?' he said.

'Karel, where is Holan?' Papa panted. 'There's a deer the size of a calf.'

'I wouldn't do it,' Prosek warned. 'The Germans passed by this afternoon on the way to the gamekeeper's house. A whole group with sub-machine guns around their necks.'

'You said you'd lend me your dog.'

'*If* he'd go with you. Holan!' Holan crawled out from under the firewood, stood up and looked at Prosek. 'You go with him,' Prosek instructed, 'and do as you're told. Understand?' Prosek turned to Papa. 'When the time comes, take his head in your hands and say, *Holan, Run!* You won't have anything else to worry about.'

Then he went into the cottage and closed the door so that Holan would understand that, for now, he had a new master. Holan sat down and observed Papa's muddy clothing as if he had never seen such an apparition in his life. But then he recognized Papa, got up and wagged his tail. Papa thought he'd won, but he was wrong. Holan sat down again, waiting for his usual treat – a couple of Prague sausages.

'Holan,' Papa pleaded, 'come with me. You remember those sausages I always brought you. Come on, pal.'

But Holan was not moved. The dog blinked and stared at Papa, but he would not follow him. He had never left Prosek to follow someone else. Though Papa begged him as he had begged no one else, the dog would not move. Papa called him 'Holan! Holan, dear!' It was pointless. Papa became so desperate that he began to feel like a madman. Taking the cloth JUDE star from his pocket, he dangled it in front of Holan.

'I'm a Jew now,' he shouted, 'and don't even have sausages for myself! I'm a Jew! I need meat for my beautiful boys, and you must get it for me!'

Weeping, he turned and headed down the path toward the island. As he walked away, he sent Prosek and Holan to hell. He vowed never to look again at the white cottage. He decided that he would pack up his tent and tools and ride home empty-handed. But as he reached a bend in the path, he couldn't resist one last look. He turned around. Holan's eyes met his. In that eternal look, the lights in each of them went out and were rekindled. No one can say exactly what passed between them, for both are dead, but even then nobody could say because they themselves could not have explained it. Maybe they cursed the dog's life, maybe the Jew's life, who can tell. Holan got to his feet, stretched, and lazily trotted after Papa like an ordinary ferryman's dog, as if he had always belonged to him.

Once on the path, Holan became that wolf. Papa hurried along the river toward the hill where the deer feasted, while Holan marched three steps ahead. Papa was a veteran of hunts, but this was unlike any he had ever taken part in. He had learned to shoot in Africa, where there was nothing to do but shoot all the time. Once near Bakov he'd brought down two woodcocks, which fly in a low zigzag pattern, with one blast of a double-barrelled shotgun. Afterwards, the country's champion marksman, Kostrba the architect, pulled a jay's feather from his cap and presented it to Papa.

Now as Papa made his way along the slope he imagined the Germans on the plain, squatting on logs beside the gamekeeper's snow-white cottage, cutting off bacon strips with daggers and drinking schnapps. He imagined them laughing while automatic machine guns bounced on their knees. He imagined them yanking out hair and whiskers from the heads and beards of Jews.

Papa knew if they caught him they'd beat him to death, shoot him to pieces, then toss him into the river where he'd float by the loveliest places he'd ever seen. He knew that a huge black boulder at Sima's Rock would block him, and there the eels would slither into him, gobbling up his innards, heart, and brain, repaying him for all the times he'd pulled their kin out of the most beautiful river in the world.

Closing in on the island, thrashing through hornbeams, they hurried on past a cluster of weak birches with their leaves a sickly swamp color and a stand of oak. Then Holan suddenly pulled up. He had spotted the deer. At that moment, even then, they might go back. Holan would have obeyed. Instead, Papa took the dog's head in his hands and whispered that killer sentence: *Holan, Run!* And Holan ran, almost flying through the last oaks. Then he ducked down, disappearing from Papa's view as he crawled through the tall grass. Papa was fascinated. Forgetting all precaution, forgetting that he might scare off the deer, he kept on walking after Holan. Finally, he saw the dog hurtle forward and he heard the deer bleating. Holan, who hadn't hunted like this in many years, simply missed. Jumping on the deer's back, the dog skidded down on his behind. Papa pulled up out of breath and leaned against an oak, watching the noisy drama. The animals were rasping, the slope was sliding, old branches were crackling, and birds screamed from the tree-tops. The deer was even larger than he had appeared to be from the island. The buck bounded toward the river as if shot from a spring, but about twenty meters from the water's edge Holan leapt for a second and last time. The deer somersaulted like a hare stricken by small bullets. But he was not dead. The two animals rolled down the hill, smearing blood on the green grass of a late spring. At last the deer lay by the river as Holan stood over him.

Papa drenched in sweat from head to toe, left the oak and wanted to descend to the river. Suddenly, he saw two men chasing the dog away. Shaking, he thought of those German machine gunners who were probably not in front of the gamekeeper's snow-white cottage anymore. But the men shooing Holan away were fishermen. Papa noticed that they had rods slung over their shoulders as others carried rifles. Unsheathing their knives, they boldly set about skinning the deer as if he belonged to them. Meanwhile, Holan returned to Papa and put his ears back, as dogs will after getting a beating, and looked up at him with guilty eyes. Sad, both of them dragged back to the ferry where Karel Prosek noticed the empty rucksack and welcomed them with barely concealed joy.

'So the horned beast has fled?' he asked.

Papa told him what had happened. Uncle Prosek never could stand it when somebody snatched a fish from a line, let alone a felled deer. He saw too that he was involved in something, regardless of his desire not to be. He was angry now.

'Listen to me!' he said. 'You walk along the high path, I'll be below you. Pretend you are looking for something. Move quickly! We leave the dog here!'

Walking quickly, almost running, they soon reached the slope of the dead deer. Papa could hear Prosek shouting.

'Forester! It was over here!'

Papa caught on and quickly responded like a bad amateur actor.

'Yeah! I think that's it!'

They listened for a moment and heard the stamping of feet. Then they saw the fishermen sprinting along the river toward Rozvedcik where the barbel usually fed in the shallow current and where they could wade the river and keep running all the way to Tramtarie.

Prosek walked to the deer and saw that he was already gutted, skinned and stuffed with fir branches, just as they did with venison in the store. Obviously, the fishermen were experts. Nearby lay the head with its magnificent antlers, its eyes closed. Prosek gazed off in the direction of the fishermen.

'Many thanks, lads,' he said.

As they stuffed the deer into the rucksack, they heard the first shots echoing in the woods. The Germans had started to hunt. Papa and Uncle Prosek ran back up the path, taking turns carrying the heavy rucksack. Back at the ferry house, they hid the rucksack in the attic, and Papa slept his last night on the island. But he didn't really sleep. All night he watched the silent stars and clear moon, listened to the river flowing past and an otter fishing somewhere. He was happy that he was there and had done what he hoped to do.

In the morning before sunrise, Papa left the ferry, but not before poor Prosek brought him a hundred cigarettes from somewhere. He strapped flour, butter, cakes, and deer meat onto Papa's bicycle rack. Papa left the antlered head to his friend, walked slowly up the hill, and rode the winding road down into Krivok-lat.

The town was swarming with Germans. Losing his nerve, Papa thought of ditching the bicycle and running away, but a woman stopped him.

'Sir,' she said, 'there's blood all over you.'

This Czech woman, whose name he never knew, took Papa home where she and her husband rewrapped the deer, made coffee to refresh him for the road, and washed the spots from his coat. Then my sly Papa sped away feeling calm again, thinking of all he had been through in the woods. He knew that today and tomorrow he'd be lucky. He rode along as if he were on a pleasant outing, and when he'd been passed without being recognized by an armored Wehrmacht car, he began to hum legion songs – even that naughty German one:

Der Elefant von Indien,
der kann Loch nicht findien.

Summer had begun. Cherry blossoms had fallen, pear and apple trees had started to shed their flowers, and fruit started to grow in that third year of the war.

When Papa arrived back in Bustehrad, the deer was justly divided. We presented one leg to the baker, Blaha, who had shown us kindness, and one to the Burgrs on their farm, who had been kinder still. Mama marinated the rest in a lovely barrel and prepared sauces and steaks, her specialties, for my brothers Hugo and Jirka. The boys stuffed themselves in order to endure the years at Terezin, Auschwitz, and Mauthausen, the death marches in freezing weather, carrying rocks up the Mauthausen steps in searing heat, and other delights dreamed up for them by the Germans. Hugo came back to us more or less okay but Jirka, who had been in Mauthausen, weighed only forty kilos and for six months died many deaths from hunger and suffering before he began to live again. Jirka never said much about what happened to him. Only once did he say 'That deer may actually have saved my life. Maybe those last morsels of substantial meat were just enough to last me till the end.'

Meanwhile, Uncle Prosek had mounted the deer's head above his cottage door in spite of his reservations about calling attention to himself. He'd insist to foresters that the beautiful antlers had come from the Alps, but he told his children and grandchildren that, overall, the hunt for that one deer had been more dangerous than all of the African hunts for wild game. Prosek promised that he'd tell them all about it one day. He never got around to it. He never carried the antlers, as he'd promised, to Krivoklat castle, either. Because Holan had died, someone stole them. Uncle followed Holan, dying soon after the war's end.

When I arrived for his funeral, a band on shore was playing a song about a faithful ferryman. Some men lowered his large black casket into his oldest boat, a boat in which he had ferried scores of dead friends to the Nezabudice side. I was old enough to know what was happening, and I wept as I never had in my life. Prosek lay in the box, his lovely mustache under his nose, as pale as Aunt Death herself. As we ferried across, the river flowed under us as it had for millions of years. I couldn't calm down. I knew that we were not burying Uncle Prosek alone. We were also laying to rest all the finest associations of my childhood. With Prosek we were burying a real English soccer ball, cold buttermilk, pickled fish and marinated deer meat, Prague sausages, Holan the dog, and the phonograph recording of 'A Thousand Miles.'

They Can Even Kill You

The two ponds in Bustehrad were separated by a dam, some poplars, and a road. The new pond never attracted me. Its shores of stone and brick were so cold. The old pond was different. Parts of its shoreline were covered with duckweed. It smelled good, too, like the brook that flowed around Oplt's pub into it. The pond smelled of manure draining from farm buildings; its waters also released the aroma of old willows and mud, mud in which carp lounged, resting their bellies. It smelled like beer from the nearby brewery, too.

In my mind's eye, newly cultivated carp swam there. I couldn't forget the perch from Krivoklat and the fighting barbels I worked so hard to catch. Fish swam in my blood. Oh, how I wanted to fish again!

But one could not fish in Bustehrad. There were no decent brooks or rivers. There were only ponds with warnings that fishing was forbidden. Over at the old pond I watched carp loaf fearlessly in the shallows. Obviously, they thought of nothing, swimming leisurely from place to place or darting in nervous troops. They ate traveling in circles, as the poplar and willow shadows bent down to my pond. Climbing the willow tree I spoke to them in a hushed voice, and it seemed to me that they pricked up their ears and listened. They were a beautiful brassy gold, and when they executed somersaults and headstands, I saw their fat yellow bellies. The brewery workers had been feeding those fish on brewer's grains!

At that time we needed delicious fat carp meat. We had so little to eat and nothing much to barter. We could trade carp for flour, bread, and Mama's cigarettes. Mama and I lived alone at that time, for the rest of the family was in a concentration camp. It was up to me to catch the carp, but it took me some time getting to know them. I had to learn to tell the difference between their good and bad moods; I had to learn how to tell when they were hungry, when they were full, and when they felt like playing. I had to recognize where they were likely to swim, and where I would look for them in vain.

I had made a firm, short rod and outfitted it with a line, float, and hook. But I couldn't begin until I knew my enemies. Not fish, people. From the castle windows I could hear the sweet German song 'Lily Marlene' on the phonograph as carp was served at their banquet. Several informers lived in the town, and they kept their windows open wide to hear everything and nothing. Bustehrad was also the home of Frantisek Zaruba, the first Fish Warden I had ever met. His job was to look after the carp; my job was to get to know him as well as I knew the fish. When was he in a good mood, and when was he in a bad one? When did he eat? When did he inspect the ponds, and when did he avoid them? I had to know all this. So I watched him. Pulling my grandfather's old cap down over my head and looking awkward in his worn suit, I limped nearby and watched Zaruba, affecting my mild disguise so that I would not make a strong impression on him.

When I first saw the man I was stunned. He was a hunchback like that poor Quasimodo, the Notre Dame bellringer in Paris. He was short, too. He could neither take long steps nor jump, and he certainly couldn't run fast. He would never catch me! But Mama warned me that some people like Zaruba can be very mean, revenging themselves on others for being marred by God. In the woods on the way to Drin, I would practice running away from Zaruba.

Then one evening I went down to see if the carp had not changed their habits. I watched for quite a while, and from time to time dark shadows flitted under the willow. The next day, I arrived with the short rod under my coat. Josef Oplt, the pub owner, stood on the dam and watched me with his one good eye (the other eye was glass). I greeted him politely but prayed to myself: 'Dear God in heaven, don't betray me. Also Mr Oplt, please don't betray me. Remember, my grandfather Ferdinand played whist in your pub and left lots of money there. At least that's what grandmother Malvina used to say. Amen.'

I climbed up into the willow tree and took out my

rod. Molding dough around the hook, I created a tempting ball. It was quiet around the pond and I couldn't be easily spotted. The stacks of the brewery belched out their smoke as beer simmered in the vats. The brook smelled delicious, and the willows rustled in the breeze. The Germans shut the castle windows because it was getting chilly. The squealers crept into their homes for the night.

Zaruba was at his dinner by the time my first carp struck. The float pirouetted like a ballerina, then dove into the water and darted beneath a willow. I jerked at the line and felt a strong pull. It was courageous, that fish. It fought well, jiggling my short rod, but in the end it gasped for air and gave up. It was beautiful. All brassy gold, its yellow belly was stuffed with grain from the brewery. I quickly hooked another and landed it, then cleared out like a cat with its catch. I couldn't take a chance by staying any longer. Passing Mr Oplt, I noticed that he was smoking a cigarette. He was silent.

Back home Mama gave me a big kiss for catching those carp. After all, the war was in its fourth year and there was little food. But, poor soul, she couldn't guess that this fishing of mine would only end in catastrophe.

They found out about me soon enough. Someone talked. Someone skulking behind those informers' windows tipped off Zaruba. I felt spider webs closing in on me, and I saw the clouds above my old pond. Ruffled by the wind, its waves threatening the grassy shore, the pond began to seem wicked to me. The brewery loomed ominously, and its stench troubled me. I caught more carp, but I was frightened. Most of our family was already imprisoned. Or they were dead. My Grandmother Malvina, who had scolded Grandfather Ferdinand for playing cards, was gassed at Auschwitz. At night in my cold bed I closed my eyes and saw a gray Heinkel with black crosses on its wings, dropping bombs. Then I would get up, go in my slippers through that terribly large, damned, dead house. I would tiptoe around my small sleeping Mama, who suffered so only because she had married a Jew before God and didn't want to part with him in this world. I would study her, the premature wrinkles on her brow, her reward for working so hard each day in the field. Perhaps she had not eaten that day. She looked so frail, so like a small child, that I began to feel like the adult. I was the sole man left in the house. Walking softly down the stone steps to the ground floor, I passed doors behind which only the sound of the dead lived. At one time, Miss Hassoldova from the post office lived there. She rests now in Bustehrad cemetery. Everywhere I looked I saw spider webs and spiders with crosses on their backs. In the cellar I looked down into the stone barrel where my last carp swam. He drove back and forth in short bursts, and each time his dull snout collided with the stone wall, he'd come back again. He paid no attention to me, as if he knew that I would only tell him fairy tales about paradise in this world, then deceive him like others who promised so much. Tomorrow I'll go back to the pond and try to catch a brother and sister for him. The three will have eyes of gold that shine like lanterns.

The following evening, after the castle windows were shut and Zaruba had sat down to his dinner, I took up my short rod and went to the dam. I passed by the poplars shedding their leaves, and Mr Oplt who stood near the dam and chainsmoked. From my willow perch I caught the first carp. He surfaced, swallowed the dough, then dove like a submarine. But I bagged him and covered him with a rag so he wouldn't splash around. As I dropped my line for another, Zaruba appeared. So he was not having his dinner. He was there at the pond, and he ran toward me from the well.

'Stop! Stop! You scoundrel!' he shouted.

He was heavy and slow, and I ran like a racehorse. Coming up to Oplt who stood under the trees, I saw him point to the open gate in his yard.

'Lock yourself in the barn!' he said.

I did, and soon I heard Zaruba arguing with Oplt. I also heard brother carp breathing in the bag, though I myself couldn't breathe. I was terribly scared. People like Zaruba are evil. They can even kill you.

An hour later Oplt opened the barn door and told me to go home safely. I came back the next day because I thought that nobody would think I'd have such nerve. Oplt was nowhere to be seen. Obviously, he wanted nothing more to do with it. Well, just as I settled into the willow, Zaruba showed up. He held a short stick, a club, with which he could beat the brain of a kid like me to a pulp. I immediately understood that Zaruba was as wise and shrewd as Quasimodo. I saw that he was more dangerous than the Germans in the castle or the informers in their open windows. He knew my habits and understood that I had poacher's blood in my veins. I'd never be able to run away from him. He'd catch me in the end with his short hard stick and beat me senseless or kill me. I let him come closer.

'Stop!' he shouted. 'You bastard! Stop, you shitty Jew!'

The insult didn't hurt. I had gotten used to them during the war. I leapt down from the willow, ran lightly across the dam, and disappeared among the poplars. I felt as light as a feather and knew he couldn't catch me. I was the only one left in my family without shackles on his ankles and chains around his neck. So I ran like a free bird through the fields. I ran along the path all the way to the blue woods. There I listened to owls through the night and slept under the fir trees. When I got back to my house in the morning, Mama told me how the police with rifles and bayonets had come to get me. She began to cry. Kneeling in front of me, she begged me never to go to the pond.

The police did not come back. Sergeant Knesl, who knew us, said that Zaruba had announced at the station:

'I'll settle this matter with that brat! It's *my* business. I'm the Fish Warden here!'

I began to make a wide circle around the pond, telling myself that crocodiles and sharks swam there. I imagined octopi pulling me down into the deep water, emitting blue ink so that Mama could not find and bury me in a silent grave next to Miss Hassoldova at Bustehrad cemetery. The pond ceased to exist for me. I forgot it and devoted my time to soccer and the woods. I had work to do, too. I gleaned and threshed grain from wheat ears; I gathered coal from coal piles for our winter fuel.

But one day (I don't know how it happened), I went down to the cellar and picked up my rod again. I felt dizzy. What a fool I'd been! There were never sharks and octopi in the old pond. But there had always been hundreds of little brother carp with golden eyes. I couldn't stand it. I went out at twilight, past the poplars, to the dam where nobody stood. Maybe I left too early; it was still light enough to see. But I was on my way and wouldn't turn back. I didn't stop at the willow but continued on as far as the pump on the pond's shore. From there I could see Zaruba should he come. Three access roads led to me. One curled around the pond, the second came up on the opposite side, and a third wound narrowly up to the school. No matter how he might come, I had two escape routes.

I unwrapped the rod and cast out. I felt exquisitely happy as the float bobbed on the surface. The water smelled fishy and looked as green as forest grass. Frogs croaked in the shallows and the steady roar of the brewery machines sounded in the distance. Then the float began to shake. As I stared at the water, I realized that something wasn't right.

Lifting my head, I was petrified. A man I did not know quietly approached down one path. From the other end of the pond another came toward me. I threw the rod in the water. My legs felt like lead. The silence of the pond was deafening, and my heart sounded an alarm. I took off. Jumping over the pump's edge, I ran up the path toward the school. It was my third and only chance. I stretched my legs, feeling the terrible silence of the town all around me. Maybe the whole town was watching my race and rooting for me. From the castle's open windows Germans peered out through binoculars. Bony little men and their matrons leaned out the informers' windows. I ran harder, then turned into the last curve.

As I rounded the bend, Zaruba stood in the middle of the road like the black Gestapo men who searched our house from time to time. The dreaded club was in his hand. Both sides of the road were flanked by high walls. No one could see us. My knees sagged. He grabbed me by the hand. Expecting a blow from the club, I ducked. But nothing happened. I looked up at him.

'Shout!' he ordered emphatically. At first, I was bewildered. 'Damn it! Scream!'

And then I understood. He wanted me to scream for the Germans and the informers listening at their windows. I imitated the squealing of a pig I had seen killed at my grandfather's. They had shot it with a Browning, but it hadn't died from the first shot, or the second. I screamed now for real, just as I had run before. Zaruba stood by the wall, whipping the air with his club. Then he shook me.

'That's enough,' he said. We faced each other. We were the last two people in this town – he marked by God, I branded by the supermen. 'What about your Papa,' he said. 'Does he write to you from the concentration camp?' I shook my head no. 'And your brothers?' I shook my head again. Then Zaruba calmly leaned against the wall as if at a spa promenade and lit a cigarette. 'Don't go to the old pond anymore,' he said. 'The new pond is lovely, too. You fish from behind farm buildings there. No one will see you. It's safe there. The new pond carp are even tastier, I think. But go there only when it's dark, when the moon isn't out.' I was dumbstruck. I nodded my agreement. 'Go now. Limp all the way home, just as you limped when we first met and you had that big cap pulled over your ears so I could not recognize you. You know, when you were first studying me.' I smiled at him. That smile was all I had to give. As I left I heard him say, 'And add some anise to the dough. The carp like it that way and bite faster.' I limped up the street.

Meanwhile, Zaruba set off down to the old pond, lashing his club about and whistling the tune 'Lily Marlene.' That song truly was lovely. Its only fault was that the SS men loved it so much. I walked home

limping. Passing the new pond, I could see carp playing in the evening light, making large circles on the
surface like the wheels of wagons or wheelbarrows.
Surely they would go for the anise-dough. All I had
to do was wait a few days for some dark nights.

Long Mile

The end of the war was in the air. Both of the Bustehrad ponds had been fished out, the carp eaten. Even the carp fry, like the ammunition, was running short, which is why the ponds were not restocked. It is difficult to restock a pond with nothing. The ponds lay barren and nobody seemed to care, what with other troubles that seemed to surface daily. Only I missed the fish. So I roamed the countryside searching for the brooks that flowed slowly through the black soil. They were as dark as the night sky around Kladno, as black as the coal from the Fran mine, not silver like a queen's ribbon or necklace. Only some of them provided homes for thin gudgeons and small sand eels. If one is very hungry, one eats such fish raw, just like the gold miners in the stories of Jack London. Silver roaches looked like sugar-coated tinsel hanging from a Christmas tree. Now and then under grassy spots on the banks I'd uncover little creatures like small crayfish. They would furiously flap their tails at me, irritated because I had pulled them from their shallow holes. There was nothing more substantial to eat, just what was found in this large aquarium. Instead of glass, its walls were the two banks, the sand bottom, and sky above. And all around forget-me-nots bloomed, insisting that we remember.

I remembered my brothers, Hugo and Jirka. Long ago we slept in two beds in a cold room, and every night I would scratch Jirka's back; he couldn't go to sleep until I had done so. He used to give me a crown for the service. And Hugo, the noble aristocrat, would make clacking sounds with his mouth to show us how Konicek's mill worked. He had been showing up there as a free hand, a stooge really, just for some flour and a kind word. He unloaded grain and emptied sacks. Then, with an old cart and bike, he would take bread around to the farmers. Usually, he had to push his bike up and down the hills so that the cart wouldn't hit him. The farmers enjoyed fine bread, and the scent of it trailed along after Hugo, wherever he rode. Many nights Hugo would sleep in the mill on a bunk after dining on bread, beer cheese, and homemade ale.

The night before Hugo left for the concentration camp, I awoke to find his handsome face leaning over me. He pressed my face between his hot hands and whispered a secret.

'When the worst times hit,' he said, 'go to Konicek's mill and bring home the old carp. They forgot him when they were clearing out the pond. Perhaps he hid among the roots. Nobody knows about him now except me – and you. He's a bearded fellow, and he swims on the side of the pond under the old willow. I used to feed him bread, but we won't be needing each other anymore. Throw some bread out and he'll swim to you.'

Months had passed since then, and I wondered sometimes what Hugo was up to. Perhaps he delivered the dead for burning; maybe instead of bread, his cart was filled with corpses, tattooed with numbers no good to them here on earth or in heaven. The Lord supposedly takes us to heaven in a different order. But we still lived there – Mama and I. And it was time for me to fetch the old carp from the mill pond, the old carp with four whiskers, which meant that he was either very wise or very stupid. I carried in my pocket a chunk of home-made bread, which the wife of Blaha the baker had given me. I nibbled on it once or twice, but managed to control myself and save most of it for the carp. I had always wanted to go to the mill, for I imagined it as the setting of a fairy tale where the Pacufraks, the little people, lived. I had spent weeks preparing, and when I set out I hummed that song my Mama had taught me:

> *Walking along the brookside,*
> *fishing for small fish,*
> *small fish are right for fishermen,*
> *and girls are right for miller-men,*
> *and prettier girls for brewery men –*
> *and all the boys are proud, oh!*

Marching past the castle beside the Lidice fields, I looked down on the site where Lidice used to be. There laborers of the German Work Front loudly sang their anthem:

> *Wir sind die Jugend*
> *mit Hacke und Spaten.*

With hoes and spades they turned the soil so that even God wouldn't recognize it. They dynamited the pond where I used to go with the boys of Lidice, scattering its water as they scattered the church. They diverted the brook from Hrebec, and paved the roads with white marble tombstones so they could walk on the names of those who had been sleeping peacefully. And they sang and sang, stopping only to prepare more dynamite. After all, it was impossible, using only hoes and spades, to wipe out white villages from the face of the earth. The Lidice fields were all around me. Mama had worked there, and potatoes and small white flowers grew up everywhere. Potatoes even grew on the graves of executed men and boys, and when the women dug them out they resembled human hearts. That was a warning, and nobody took those potatoes home. Only the greedy Hanackova tried it, lugging a bag to her house, and she was dead within a year.

There was plenty of time to fetch the carp. The sun was low but still well above the horizon when I decided that I would go again to the Long Mile, a strip of road lined with ancient linden trees leading to the airfield. Long Mile. The name had infinite meaning for me. It meant a big race, or a long road, or the stretch of one's life.

'With perseverance, head toward your goal; you'll overcome even a long mile.'

That was what Grandfather Ferdinand used to say. I hurried on my way and pinched a few more bits of the homemade bread intended for the old carp. Crossing the brook, I climbed a hill and came to a sudden halt at the top. The Long Mile hardly existed anymore. Later, I learned that a Stuka fighter had brushed one of those lindens with its wing while coming in for a landing. It turned a somersault in the air and fell, burning, into the field. The pilot was killed in the crash before the firetruck could arrive. And the trees paid for it. A Nazi general drove up in a track vehicle and issued an immediate order.

'Off with the enemy's heads!' he shouted.

And they cut off the tops of the trees, leaving only stumps. People felt very sorry for the trees. Nearby farmers wept for those trees as if they were their own children, remembering how they had walked in their shade to the marketplace in Prague with eggs and butter. They remembered the honey season when the trees smelled sweet and seemed to rise up into heaven as the bees circled them, higher and higher. Villagers had made tea from linden blossoms to guard against winter coughs. But now horses were pulling the trunks to an open field. Though the wood was old, it was as white as a virgin's body. All the farmers could do was grumble how in the old days no soldier could cut down a living tree and escape punishment. I went all the way down that scarred Long Mile, and reaching the end of it I could almost see Prague. Then I walked back to Konicek's mill, my legs aching.

The mill itself was beautiful, almost as lovely as the mill from my childhood at Nezabudice. The attic opening was mysterious. I was certain that the Pacufraks, the little people, came into the mill through that opening when the miller left for the pub. Merry fellows all, they would joke, dance, and sing *a ring a ring o'roses* to the rhythm of the mill wheel. The oldest member of their troop, who would remember King George leading his troops into Busteves, would sit on the chimney and crow as smoke slowly escaped from under his horsetail. From his warm sitting place he could keep an eye out for the return of the tipsy miller.

When I arrived all was quiet, and it looked as if the miller was at home. I was cautious but didn't see any Pacufraks lurking about. Entering the courtyard, I knocked at the cottage door. What would the miller's name be? Since the mill was called Konicek's, that was a good guess. Then the miller himself stepped out, buttoning up his vest.

'What do you want, boy?' he asked in a kind voice.

'May I fish here, Mr Konicek?'

The miller leaned against the wall. 'I am not Konicek,' he said. 'That was the first miller's name.

You won't catch anything, but go ahead. Only perch remain, and they aren't as big as your little finger. Even my cat Lucie won't eat them. Birds dropped them off as roe, bringing them in on their beaks and legs. They won't take a hook because their mouths are too small. It's a dead pond now, just like a polluted river or mill. Listen, don't go to the pond. Come inside and talk.'

He was obviously a good man, but I shook my head and took out my line, hoping he wouldn't change his mind. He just waved his hand, but I knew better. Only I knew the secret of the pond. Me and my brother Hugo. I headed for the pond as the miller mockingly called after me.

'Everything you catch is yours! Everything!'

Then he walked into the mill. I sighed with relief and quickly arrived at the shallow pond, so small one could throw a pebble across it. Still, it was like a beautiful porcelain salad bowl. Poplars and a few willows grew along its shore, and rocking nearby was a small boat with its two oars. The water was green and clean and I could see the perch swimming, looking like tiny willow leaves. What had they offered the birds to carry them to such a lovely pond? What did they promise? Nothing. Nature took care of it. They played in the shallows like children. They were so tiny that I fancied them the playthings of a young prince in a lonely castle. I had other worries, however. I hurried down to the cracked willow where the old carp supposedly lived. What if the miller had already caught him? He had laughed as I left, saying that whatever I caught would be mine. (Hadn't he also shouted that should I find anything he would add to it? What would he give me? Half the mill and his sweet daughter?)

The willow leaned over the water, brushing the surface with its narrow leaves, but I couldn't see any fish. I set to work tying a hook to a long line, then attached a quill from a goose that Papa had killed. Then I cut a rod. Making a ball of bread in my fists, I baited the hook and cast the line. The homemade bread still retained its aroma. I was terribly hungry, but that bread was not for me. It belonged to the old carp. Working it in my hands, I had broken it like a communion wafer. Pieces of bread created small islands on the pond's surface. They floated along but nothing else happened. I began to talk in a low, quiet voice.

'Little carp. Hey, old man. Swim up. It's me, Hugo's brother. You remember Hugo. He fed you the home-made bread. Little carp . . .'

I felt good again, fishing publicly after so many years. I did not miss the fish wardens. As time went by, I had trouble keeping my eyes open. Walking the Long Mile had exhausted me; so on I slept huddled like a badger. When I finally woke up the sunset reflected off the pond. The rod was lying beside me, and the goose quill had not moved. The surface was swept clean. The bread had disappeared. I thought immediately of the old carp. So he had eaten the bread, greased his whiskers, but shrewdly left the line as it was. He did not wish to leave Konicek's pond. I imagined him opening his big trap to swallow the bread on the surface while I slept. I threw out the last pieces of bread and dozed off again. I dreamt of the Long Mile, of the airplane burning. I saw the pilot burning in his overalls and I was sorry for him even though he was a German.

When I woke up again my rod was moving through the water and a big carp was pulling it along behind him. I didn't waste much time! Stripping off my clothes, I plunged into the cold water. The mud squished through my toes on the bottom and my private parts shrunk. I set out after the carp. Redfinned perch splashed in every direction like colored leaves, and the water quickly turned muddy. It wasn't easy! The rod pulled away from me like some strange ship without passengers. When I started to gain a little, the carp sped up, too, splashing and churning up the surface. I continued the chase, hoping to tire him out. Then the miller appeared at the dam.

'What are you doing?' he shouted.

'I'm chasing a carp that's made off with my rod!' I yelled.

'A carp? Get out of the water!'

As I climbed out he was already returning from the mill with a large landing net and a flour sack. Noticing how my teeth chattered, how my skin turned blue, green, and all the colors of the rainbow, he threw me the flour sack.

'Dry yourself,' he said. 'It's terrible to look at you.'

I toweled off, turning white from the remains of the flour. Meanwhile, the miller was down at the pond untying the small boat. Throwing the net into it, he motioned for me to get in. I was happy to have his help at that point. He leaned into the oars and we shot off after the carp. The miller, who was very strong, made the boat jump on the surface, almost as if it sailed through the air. But the carp was also strong, and the rod spooked him; and the boat and the miller did, too. Every minute or so when the carp's big dorsal fin appeared, the sweating miller would curse and call on God and the devil for aid. He quickly stripped off his vest. Then the carp made a mistake. Panicking, he swam into a small corner of the pond from which he could not escape. The miller rowed us up to the rod and I grabbed it while the carp lay on his side, breathing heavily. The miller scooped him up with the net and landed him in the boat.

On shore the miller tossed the carp out on the autumn grass, and I had my first real chance to inspect him. His whiskers were like a water sprite's. Only his pipe was missing. His eyes were peculiar, too, so wise and brown. They looked like tiny loaves of home-made bread. Otherwise, he was a golden piglet of God. As the sunset dissolved into dusk, the gold of the sun seemed to blend with the gold of the fish, weeping and flowing back into the pond. The carp's fins looked a little ragged, suggesting that he had worked hard to find things to eat when the homemade bread supply dried up. The miller was checking him over, too, but with eyes different than mine.

'Who would have guessed that such a fat fish would still be in my pond?' he said.

Then he picked up the fish, holding it like a baby in his arms, and went back down to the mill. Suddenly, I understood.

'Mr Konicek,' I said, 'that carp is mine'

He turned back to face me. 'You're too small for such a large fish,' he said.

Naked and white with flour dust, I followed him into the courtyard. I hated the thought of losing that fish. It didn't just belong to me; it belonged to Hugo, too, who had fed it bread on so many afternoons. The miller walked into a shed and dropped the fish on a board. Then he walked into the cottage. While he was gone I cradled the carp's head in my hands.

'Little carp,' I said, 'I shouldn't have come here.'

The miller returned with a mallet and knife. He bashed the carp's head in, then cut his gills so the blood would drain. Then he scraped off the large scales, which scattered in all directions, falling like gold rain to the ground, sticking to the wood and my flour-dusted body. As he split the fish down the middle and its intestines spilled to the ground, I could see clumps of my precious, undigested dirty bread. The miller kicked them toward a flock of begging hens, and I wept. The miller looked at me.

'Are you still here?' I asked if I could take the scales. 'Sure,' he said, 'and get lost. It'll be dark soon.'

Kneeling in the mud, I filled my hands with the scales. Walking over to my pile of clothes, I stuffed them into my pockets. Then it hit me – the grief and sorrow – and anger. I hated that unjust mill where the chimney already smoked as my big fish was being cooked. I walked over to the old willow. As it got darker what little light remained seemed to collect on her rotting trunk, as if welcoming someone or saying goodbye. Then I did not feel so lonely, and I felt that yes, the farmers were right when they claimed that trees are alive and as helpless as children or wild animals.

When I stopped crying I started back, but the way seemed longer than it had before. Back home Mama was already asleep. On the table a cup of goat's milk and a slice of black bread were waiting for me.

Later, I spread the scales out on the table in my room. First, I arranged them in the shape of the old carp. Then I lined them up into rows, squadrons, battalions, and issued commands: right turn – left turn! I was directing their attack on Konicek's mill! I imagined the scales, strutting and shining, as an army come to this world to enforce justice. Then I fell asleep under my feather comforter, forgiving the unjust like a king. Deeper into my dream the scales became beautiful gold coins offered by a carp king. On each coin an emperor with whiskers was embossed, the chest of his uniform cluttered with decorations. An inscription under him read: *Romanum imperarum*. I issued another command: About face! The coins turned and the Czech lion and Lothringian coat-of-arms appeared. Then I dreamt of honey time, the festival of trees, the festival of bees. In that dreamscape I saw a beautiful virgin, her body white like the lindens in the alley that was called the Long Mile.

Big Water Tramp

Papa wanted to go fishing one more time with Karel Prosek. It didn't matter what kind of fish we'd be after. When we arrived at Branov, the men embraced each other just as they had during the war after a long absence. Then Prosek climbed into the attic and brought down yellow bamboo rods, which he dusted and brushed clean of cobwebs. The rods still bore the old wheel spinning reels. Then he went off to dig earthworms in the garden. Next he placed the head of one white hen on the block and chopped it off, then gave me the bird to pluck while he poured homemade slivovitz, made from plums, into a bottle.

They decided we would climb upriver beyond the dam and catch eels. When we got hungry, we would roast the hen, and return the next morning. Papa thought that eels would make perfect presents because their meat is inimitably excellent, something like a fine tongue, certainly different altogether from the meat of river fish. Eel tastes of long distances, its fat made up of wide-ranging foods and ocean grass. Toward evening we left, each of us carrying a rod and sack to sit on, so that the ground wouldn't chill us. Uncle Prosek tossed the guts of the plucked hen to the live fish, then washed its body in cool water.

This trip reminded me of our past forays after barbel, except that the two of them were older. They walked and breathed heavily along the path. Just as it had been before the war, the sky was blue. The water tumbled over the dam and across the way the small lantern of the Nezabudice mill gave off its light.

At last Uncle Prosek said, 'We'll stay here.'

We unpacked the rods, all six of them, and positioned them next to each other. Papa hung a small bell, no larger than a child's marble, from each rod. They looked like ornaments from a Christmas tree. Each gold bell would jingle when an eel swung the rod. But it was a bad night for eels. We all knew it. The silver moon was full and bright, and the sky was dotted with white stars. An eel, like a bat or wild game, prefers the darkness and stays hidden on bright nights. But we didn't mind. It seemed more important, that night, that we were together, perhaps for the last time. Leaving the rods in peace, we walked away and Uncle Prosek started a small fire. Later, he hung the hen on a wire above it, then pulled out the bottle and repeated his command to me of ten years ago under the acacia tree.

'Have a snoot.'

I did. I was almost a man, Papa had no objections, and he had a snoot, too, even though he was never much of a drinker. The fire warmed us outside, and the slivovitz inside. We chatted all night while Papa and Uncle Prosek puffed on Egyptian cigarettes and discussed the adventures they had lived through. I don't remember exactly now, but I seem to recall some events in Africa and some beautiful women. They also talked about fish, going over old accounts, and they came to the conclusion that all fishermen arrive at: the largest fish that either had ever caught had actually gotten away. Uncle Prosek explained how once, on a path above an island, he had dropped a rope that held a live eleven-kilo pike. Rolling into the river, it chewed through the clothesline and never took his bait again.

Then a bell rang. It was an odd, strange sound under the stars, and at first we could not understand who would ring a doorbell out there. Then we remembered the gold bells and made a mad dash for the rods. Papa pulled up a one-kilo eel that had apparently mistaken a bright night for a dark night, and tossed him into a thick net. Making five knots in the top of it, he hung the net from an alder tree. Then we sat down and tore into the smokey hen, finishing it off with slivovitz. We were silent then, listening only to the night. Chubs smacked after smaller fish, and bats quietly flew in and out of the alders. Stars swam in the river and the moon looked after them, fretting over each one because Uncle Universe had consigned them to his care and would punish him if he did not protect them. I looked at my fellow creatures. They were huddled on sacks, dozing like puppies among hen bones, the bottle of slivovitz between them.

I walked down to the alder where the net hung. The eel was still alive, his gold eyes glistening as if he were a man with a fever. He started to wriggle, but his struggle was hopeless. Still, like some driven people he would not give up. Like them, though his body was dying and broken, he thought only of running away, of life.

Walking back to the camp, I lay down on the grass close to the fire and thought about that eel, the wanderer and his kin. His life, I thought, possessed more mystery than fact. I thought about fish that have inhabited this planet for millions of years, confidants of the secrets of rivers, seas, and oceans. I thought of Aristotle's erroneous notion that eels are born in the mud of a lake. I thought of Dane Schmidt defending the true theory that eels spawn near America in the Sargasso Sea after making the long journey from the rivers of Europe and Africa. Under sargasso weeds they make love in one of the world's saltiest and warmest seas. They rock their children on weeds like cradles, at depths no human has ever seen. I think that the eel prefers it that way. Man has pursued him in airplanes and in ships; he has even saddled him with primitive transmitters. But after all that, man could not find out the truth about the eel.

We do not know where they die. Maybe they perish after spawning, falling unseen to the ocean bottom to rest in its endless grave. Meanwhile, even as they die, their children, glassy translucent elvers, are caught up by the Gulf Stream and transported miles and miles away. When they grow to the size of willow leaves, they swim for three years, hunting for the rivers and estuaries where their parents lived. Once there, only the males remain in the estuary, waiting for a full-grown female to return from the rivers. There they live for decades, as if they could survive only there. And that is where we catch them, the narrow headed and the wide headed, the greenish or bluish-black. Those that escape us set off on their long pilgrimage to the Sargasso Sea. And scientists have studied them, wondering how they find their way. Birds navigate by the stars and the sun, but what do eels deep beneath the ocean surface follow? Instinct, magnetism, experience? Do they possess above-average intelligence, a finer sense of orientation?

That night by the fire it did not seem so complicated to me. I knew that eels were born near America and returned. All creatures find their way home. Eels are born near America, want to make love there, and then die in a native sea. They pursue their ambition so faithfully: they swim like mad, nothing is too great a hurdle for them. Even so, some of them travel as if blind, and some are forced by the current into turbines and are cut to pieces by the executioner's wheel. It is said that eels travel in the wet grass around big dams, overcome thousands of fishing and poaching traps, and even enlarge their eyes while at sea. They change color, too, becoming silver, as they swim toward their goal, never losing hope.

Man built dams and poured axle grease into the rivers, and eels could neither rise nor sink. Then he found that he needed eels, so he began to import them by plane in cases lined with ice and moss. He'd release these babies into the river closest to home with the hope of catching them in a few years. But who helps the strongest outwit man's snares on the journey back?

My head was splitting as I thought about this by the fire. I added no more wood since the day was breaking, and the lights in the mill had gone out. I sat there thinking of the bad things people say about eels. Contrary to what many think, eels do not have poisonous blood. Why would they? On occasion, when Papa would bring home his catch, Mama would play with an eel, stroking its belly until it stretched out like a ruler and slept. Maybe it dreamed then as children do, imagining itself a bird or a supersonic airplane, imagining that it did not have to search so long for weeds in the sea.

As dawn broke fully, Papa coughed and got up to get the rods and eels. I strolled along behind him. When we came upon the net and the alder tree, our eyes got as large as an eel's in deep water. The net was empty, dripping slime. Swaying there, it looked like a signal of defeat, a flag at half mast. With his snout, the captive had enlarged a small stitch, contracted his waist, and slipped through. Falling from the tree onto the wet grass, he dove back into the water.

'He's gone,' Papa said without cursing. Then he yawned, tired, sleepy, sore, and added, 'But it was a magical night.'

It was true even though we hadn't caught anything. I stood by the alder, gazing at the net, and thought of the eel who had not lost hope of one day seeing the Sargasso Sea.

Dried Fish

Late in his life, Papa fished less and less and seemed to be digging constantly in the garden. His success there was more obvious than at the dam. All kinds of plants blossomed and climbed skyward. When he was not in the garden, Papa was painting our cottage to make it the most beautiful home in the region.

When he did go fishing it was only to escape Mama, who ranted at him because he had prematurely attempted to retire. Down at the river he slept most of the time, just as many fishermen do. The water hums, the small waves roll as the clouds float by, and the wife is miles away. The rods are set so that the fish can almost catch themselves. Of all the sleep a man can have, the fisherman's sleep is the sweetest. It is the greatest of luxuries – sleep *and* fishing. Papa was a master at it, sleeping in a rickety boat above the railway bridge at Skochovice. His lines cast, he lay on the bottom of the boat like a tramp in his rags, paying no attention to the fact that at least twenty meters of water lay below him. Remember, Papa could not swim! To each rod he had attached an empty tin, and when a parma bit, the tin would fall and wake him. It was an inventive contraption and system, and sometimes it even earned a parma and a smile from Mama. She liked the parma because it had flaky, tough meat that was best prepared boiled, drenched with butter and sprinkled with parsley. Because of this, Papa concentrated on catching parma.

One day my brother, Hugo, arrived from Kladno. Papa had been down at the river the entire afternoon. From our house we could see only the boat and the tins, which glistened in the sunset. It looked as if the boat itself were fishing while the tins stood guard. Papa had obviously fallen asleep again in the boat's bottom, with his hunter's hat and its watchful jay's feather pulled down over his eyes to shut out the tickling sun.

'Swim out and fetch him home for supper,' Mama said to Hugo. 'He's slept enough.'

Down at the river, Hugo stripped off his clothes and dove in from the dam. Swimming beautifully, just like our brother Jirka, he would have made their teacher, Uncle Jirka Vodicka (who trained many great European swimmers before the war) proud. As Hugo paddled up to the boat, he heard Papa snoring loudly enough to discourage fish anywhere. Grabbing the boat, Hugo rocked it.

'Papa, time to float home,' he said.

'What would I do at home?' Papa asked, climbing out of his sleep. He had caught no parma that day and was in no hurry to leave his fishing hole, where he had no shortage of lemonade (which Mama in disgust called piss). Turning over, Papa dozed again.

Meanwhile, Hugo swam around the boat inspecting the rods. He noticed that something wasn't right. The rods were not bent over the water. They soared straight up like power poles, their lines ending on the bridge. Hugo had seen nothing like that in his life. Had Papa really thrown the small bait in a curve, stranding it on the railway bridge? They had been drying up there all day. Papa, who did not see well anymore, had not noticed and had not checked the rods. He slept on and on like a baby, or a very tired old man content to dream on in peace. Climbing into the boat, Hugo pulled the bait off the bridge and reeled them in. Waking up, Papa protested.

'What are you up to? Sunset is the best time to catch the biggest parma. Mama likes them.'

Hugo almost impulsively replied that the parma would have to grow wings and fly up to the bridge to find the bait where only the Paris-Dobris Express traveled. But he checked himself, saying nothing. It was sad. Papa had once been a great fisherman, but up on that bridge he could only catch a train. If it could be a train pulling into the station of Youth, then that would be beautiful. But no train stops there. More likely there is a stop in a train station called Heaven.

Speaking softly, Hugo said: 'Papa, let's sail home. We have sausages and paprika waiting, and you love them.'

Only hot sausages could lift Papa out of the bottom of the boat when he hoped to land a big parma. He rubbed his eyes and began to pull up the anchor stones with a winch. Then he bent his back to the oars and his rickety boat crept into its home port.

Rabbits with Wise Eyes

Mama and Papa sold their cottage and bought a small house in Radotin that had an apple tree blossoming above its roof. It was to be their last post here on earth, and it was a happy one. Though they labored and lived in a foolish dream about the Messiah one day taking care of them, they worked more than they dreamed, so it was not so bad. Papa's itch for other women had passed, and a kind of serenity had set in. The only problem was a familiar one. There was never enough money.

Papa came up with yet another scheme to make a fortune, this time with the help of rabbits. He bought rabbits, gave rabbits away, sold rabbits, and worked harder than he had ever worked before, building elaborate hutches for them, which he decorated with curtains. They looked like mansions for long-eared nobility.

Eventually he got into raising a special breed, Champagne rabbits, which were the color of American rockets taking off for the moon. At times they seemed more silver than gray, at times the reverse, and for rabbits they had beautiful and wise eyes, as if they knew the answer to everything. Papa whiled away the hours chatting with them and rubbing them under their chins. I cannot recall clearly that the rabbits loved him.

Each dawn and evening he would cut fresh grass for them. He got up so early that the region was still asleep and the grass was not yet wilted. He performed this twice daily ritual as if it were a hallowed ceremony. At dawn the green stalks were bright with dew and the wild rabbits gamboled on the coal dumps. Occasionally, an early rising peasant would shout a greeting, for everyone knew Papa, as he knelt down on one knee to wield his well-sharpened sickle, which never chewed grass. Lowering it to the ground, the sickle hissed as he gathered the grass into bouquets, one for each rabbit, as if each were a lady in a front row seat. Then he hitched the cart to himself and pulled it along as he whistled. Back home, he would stuff the grass into the hutches, waking the still sleeping rabbits.

'Good morning, boys. Here's something yummy.' Naturally, he overfed the rabbits, scraping out tons of manure, almost as much manure as the feed he had brought in. Still, the rabbit hutches were amazingly clean.

He would brag to his friends, 'You can't believe it, can you? You idiots could eat in there!'

Meanwhile, Mama successfully raised turkeys and hens and sold their eggs. They went on like this for almost ten years. Papa became friendly with the gardeners from the nearby Waltrovka factory and would bring home the most beautiful roses. On the way home he always forgot their names, so he would name them after presidents and best friends like Beda Peroutka and Karel Prosek. Those roses had strong leaves and stems, and waxen blooms that seemed to reach right up to heaven. Papa could not bring himself to cut them, for he could not bear to see a flower fall to the ground, so that task was left to Mama. When she did so, Papa would retreat to the back of the garden, with its view of the Zbraslav chateau, and tend his gladiola beds. Nearby, he also cultivated strawberries, currants, and gooseberries, and hidden from the, sun in a concrete pool he watched over the green eels with wicked eyes, which he caught in Berounka.

One winter when the snow rose to the lip of the windows, he set traps for the ravens. No matter the time of day, Papa would run out, even in slippers, when he heard a snared raven flapping its wings.

In those days many wise people from Prague would visit him, and he would serve them soup made out of the cagey ravens. Then he would tell them about his rich relatives, the Poppers and Abeleses, farmers from Horsovsky Tyn. They had all fled to Canada before the war, and they were so rich, according to Papa, that they had taken with them their Swiss shepherds and Swiss cows.

Often we dreamed of their caravan, as lovely as a

painting by Ales; we imagined our uncles Hugo and Alois riding on a passenger train with their Swiss shepherds in funny hats and Swiss cows with horns like the ones painted on chocolate bars peering out of the freight car windows behind them. We imagined banners decking the sides of the cars like those decorating the cars of the Busch or Humberto circus.

But as we discovered later, the truth was somewhat different. Our rich relatives had only one Swiss shepherd, Mr Schnocker, and no cows at all. They acquired farms in Canada, but they worked hard to do it, and labor still to the present day. Their children grew up to be professors, like Vilma Iggers who began by milking cows. Later she worked in a candy factory, then graduated from college and got a job as a lecturer at a university.

But Papa had no wish to dwell on truth from a foreign country, and that was beautiful. When he talked about the Canadian Abeleses and Poppers, his eyes lit up as he insisted that they must own half of Canada by now, including the lakes and rivers. One day, he was certain, they would invite him to go salmon fishing.

In those days, Papa loved to talk all the time. The saddest story he told took place during the war, when he had to take our dog, Tamik, and old Mrs Loewy's cat to Prague to hand over to the authorities because Jews were not allowed to have pets. On the bus the cat took a shit from fear, and Papa had to leave the bus and wash her in the snow. Reaching Prague on foot in the afternoon, he spent hours walking around the city. He took them out of the box in front of the castle, in the Old Town Square where twenty-seven Czech noblemen had been executed. He also gave his food to the dog and cat that day and went hungry.

Those ten years passed as quickly as the ripples from a pebble tossed in his beloved Bustehrad pond.

Then one day a member of the rabbit breeders club told him that if he tattooed his Champagne rabbits, he might very well win prizes and money at the next show. The notion appealed to him.

Soon, he called in an expert rabbit tattooer. It was a terrible job, what with hundreds of rabbits. The expert had to imprint certain numbers in their ears. Only then could a rabbit become a pure thorough-bred. It was like the process of a gentleman acquiring a pedigree. Papa watched over the rabbits for days, dreaming that he would sell most of them at the next exhibition. Then rabbit breeders throughout the region would raise them, telling everyone that they were from old Popper.

The Novaks, his friends from an agricultural co-operative, loaned him their small display cases, and with his last money Papa rented a truck. He rose early to load the rabbits, but before he left he took Mama's hand and walked with her into the pantry. In recent years that room had housed little more than some flour, rice, barley, a bottle of oil, and some candles and matches. It had always depressed Papa, for before the war he had always been proud that his pantry was well stocked. Opening the door, he said, 'Herma, give it a good wash! We shall fill it soon. Put clean paper in here!' Then he kissed her once for luck, as if he were going off to war and was certain of victory.

Then he drove off to Karlstejn, imagining that he would sell all the rabbits and take only a few home for future breeding. Most of all, he intended to return with the beautiful male, Michael.

When the judges examined his rabbits at last, Papa felt his heart constrict as if they were judging his own children. They weighed the rabbits, blew into their fur, and inspected them. Then they informed him that he had not properly manicured and pedicured them. He had not washed their privates, and this was a serious shortcoming. No prizes could be awarded to him. Of course, this also meant that nobody would buy his rabbits.

Papa turned pale. 'You bastards!' he shouted. 'So that's the way it is! You don't like Jews!' Suddenly the entire show fell silent, and even the rabbits seemed to bend down their ears in shame. Then one rabbit breeder, hoping to cheer Papa up, addressed him with the traditional breeders' greeting.

'Friend Pavel!' he said. 'For a long time, we had called the magical spirits of the countryside the Pavels, and somewhere along the line we had told ourselves that since we lived in a Czech country we should have a true Czech name instead of Popper. Maybe we were a little more cowardly than was necessary.'

'I am a shit friend to you!' Papa shouted at that

breeder. He sat down, defeated, waiting for something to save him. Maybe his son Jirka, who had often helped him with his Fiat, or his son Hugo, who was good with his hands, would appear. Or perhaps our uncles Hugo and Alois would fly in with the best Canadian rabbits so that Papa could out-trump everybody. Or maybe Uncle Ota would arrive, who worked in northern Bohemia after the war, and whom we loved as much as Aunt Helenka from Prague.

But nothing happened, and no one came. Finally, it grew dark. The rabbit breeders packed up and left, and Papa remained sitting there alone. Eventually, he stood up and hauled all of the rabbit crates through a hole in a fence into a green field and opened all of the gates. Slowly the stunned rabbits crawled out. They had never seen the sky above them or felt growing alfalfa under their bellies.

'Run, boys,' Papa told them. But they didn't run. They were used to Papa, and they crawled back to his feet and rubbed against them like cats. He tried chasing them away, but they wanted to be with him. They knew that life would never be so good again, that the grass would never be as delicious as it was back in their beautiful hutches where they lived like princes in a castle. They did not care if Papa's honest ignorance had conspired against them to rob them of prizes.

In the end, he ran away from them. His beloved Michael kept up with him the longest, but Papa finally outran him, too. Arriving at the railway station, he reached into his pockets but found only a handful of crumpled cigarettes.

Then he saw the river, which for him was everything in life. He walked down to the water and followed it in the direction of his wife and his home. The moonlight transformed the river into a silver road, and here and there Papa stretched out on the grassy banks, resting his aching body.

For the first time in his life Papa walked such a long way without whistling or singing. He did not even sing that favorite legion song about elephants, or the song about the red scarf. It was as if a spring in a record player had broken, as if the movie musical about the happy tramp and the fisherman had gone dark. Walking on, he looked up at the sky and saw, now and then, a pantry lined with clean paper. Then he saw a fish close to shore, a fish with large bulging eyes. They faced each other, and Papa thought that the fish must be very wise and very old, for no other fish had killed it and no fisherman had caught it. Afterwards, he insisted that the fish had come up to look at him because he had killed thousands of fish during his own lifetime. Then the fish wagged its fins and swam away, and Papa continued on his journey.

In the morning he limped up to the gate. Out of breath and holding his chest, he was led inside by Mama. She was frightened. Passing the pantry, he turned his head away at first, fearing the sight of clean paper, but then he looked. The pantry's paper was still dirty. Inside he saw that there was still a little flour, rice, barley, and a bottle of oil. He sat down then and smiled.

'You are my best friend,' he said to Mama. She called an ambulance, and when it arrived the attendants led Papa outside. He cursed them. Then he pulled free at the gate and ran back toward the house, shouting over his shoulder that he had forgotten something. He did not go back into the house to fetch a transistor radio, as so many people do. He had once painted a beautiful sign, which he was very proud of. In a moment, he emerged from the house with it and hung it on the gate. RETURN SOON it said. But he did not.

Epilogue

I went mad at the winter Olympics in Innsbruck. My brain got cloudy, as if a fog from the Alps had enveloped it. In that condition I came face to face with one gentleman – the Devil. He looked the part! He had hooves, fur, horns, and rotten teeth that looked hundreds of years old. With this figure in my mind I climbed the hills above Innsbruck and torched a farm building. I was convinced that only a brilliant bonfire could burn off that fog. As I was leading the cows and horses from the barn, the Austrian police arrived. They handcuffed me and took me down into the valley. I cursed them, pulled off my shoes, and walked barefoot through the snow. I was thinking of Christ as he was led to the cross. Back over the border I was delivered to the doctors in Prague.

This period wasn't so bad for me, but it was terrible for those who loved me and watched. In fact, I felt very good, and I did everything with enthusiasm and conviction. It is lovely being a Christ who administers blessings.

Then the bad times began. The doctors, with their

pills, got me into a state in which I realized I was mad. That is sadness, when you know that you are no Christ but a wretch whose brain, which makes a man a man, is sick. So they put you behind bars even though you didn't kill or hurt anyone, even though you stood for no trial. And so you begin to envy the people outside, the people who go on living.

Only a miracle can save you. I waited for one for five years, sitting alone in a chair. I won't say that I suffered like an animal, because no man knows how an animal suffers though he may often write about it. I know that I suffered terribly. There are no words to describe it. And if there were such words, people would not believe them because they do not want to hear about madness. It frightens them.

When I felt better, I tried to remember what had been beautiful in my life. I did not think about love or how I had wandered all over the world. I did not think about night flights across the ocean or how I played Canadian hockey in Prague. I remembered walking along the brooks, rivers, ponds, and dams to fish. I realized that these were the most beautiful experiences in my life.

Why? I cannot explain it exactly, but I tried to come close to it in this book. I didn't always remember where I caught which fish and how long it was from head to tail, but I remembered the rituals of fishing. Most of all I remembered how I walked or drove to the fish. At the Zelivka, I rode a rickety bike to a trout brook while everybody was still sleeping. The scene was like an open-air theater. The grass and fields glistened with dew, the birds were waking up, and close by deer grazed, acting as if they knew me. Overwhelmed by humility, I scooped up the brook water and wanted to cross myself, but I did not. I remembered an out-of-the-way dam above Janov where I used to catch trout as big as carp with my mother. There the water was as green as grass – heaven's meadow about which I had always dreamed. But most of all I thought about the Krivoklat region and the Nezabudice mill with its always burning light that shone as well for poachers as it did for cops. I thought about mysterious eels with their small snake eyes that migrated through there on their pilgrimages.

It was fascinating to me that so much had disappeared from my life but fish had remained. They were the alternative, the natural world where the jerky streetcar of civilization did not threaten to jump its tracks. Now I know that many who fish do not go out for the fish alone. They answer the tug of antiquity, the yearning to hear a bird calling or an animal growling or the leaves falling. When I was slowly dying, I remembered most the river I had loved most in my life. Before I could fish in it again I would take its water in the shell of my hands and kiss it as I would kiss a woman. Then I would splash it into my face and set up my rod.

In front of me the river flowed. A man can see the sky. He can stare into the forest, but nobody really sees into a river. Only with a fishing rod can one look there. Sometimes, when I sat at the barred window and fished in memory, the pain was almost unbearable. I had to block it out, the beauty, and I had to remind myself that dirt, foulness, and muddy waters also ran in the world. When I succeeded in this, I did not long so much for freedom.

Finally. I have found the right word: Freedom. Fishing is freedom most of all. To walk on and on after trout, drinking from natural springs, to be alone if only for an hour, a few days, weeks, months, to be free of television, newspapers, radio, the community of men and women – that is what I longed for.

I wanted to kill myself a hundred times when I felt I couldn't go on, but I never did. Maybe my desire to kiss the river and catch the silver fish again kept me going. Fishing taught me patience, and my memories helped me go on.

Contemporary ... Provocative ... Outrageous ...
Prophetic ... Groundbreaking ... Funny ... Disturbing ...
Different ... Moving ... Revolutionary ... Inspiring ...
Subversive ... Life-changing ...

What makes a modern classic?

At Penguin Classics our mission has always been to make the best
books ever written available to everyone. And that also means
constantly redefining and refreshing exactly what makes a 'classic'.
That's where Modern Classics come in. Since 1961 they have been an
organic, ever-growing and ever-evolving list of books from the last
hundred (or so) years that we believe will continue to be read over and
over again.

They could be books that have inspired political dissent, such as
Animal Farm. Some, like *Lolita* or *A Clockwork Orange*, may have
caused shock and outrage. Many have led to great films, from *In Cold
Blood* to *One Flew Over the Cuckoo's Nest*. They have broken down
barriers – whether social, sexual, or, in the case of *Ulysses*, the
boundaries of language itself. And they might – like *Goldfinger* or
Scoop – just be pure classic escapism. Whatever the reason, Penguin
Modern Classics continue to inspire, entertain and enlighten millions
of readers everywhere.

'No publisher has had more influence on reading habits than Penguin'
Independent

'Penguins provided a crash course in world literature'
Guardian

The best books ever written

PENGUIN 🐧 CLASSICS

SINCE 1946

Find out more at www.penguinclassics.com